THE SIGN.

Resigned to spinsterhood, Amy Gibbon is astounded to receive a proposal of marriage from Viscount Charles Chard upon their very first meeting! Love quickly flares in her heart, but Charles is more reticent — he needs an heir, and this is a marriage of convenience. Determined to win her new husband over, Amy follows him to the Continent, where he must search for his father's precious signet ring which was stolen at Waterloo. Can true love blossom under such circumstances?

ANNE HOLMAN

THE SIGNET RING

Complete and Unabridged

LINFORD
Leicester

First published in Great Britain in 2018

First Linford Edition
published 2019

A catalogue record for this book is available
from the British Library.

ISBN 978–1–4448–4063–6

Published by
F. A. Thorpe (Publishing)
Anstey, Leicestershire

Set by Words & Graphics Ltd.
Anstey, Leicestershire
Printed and bound in Great Britain by
T. J. International Ltd., Padstow, Cornwall

This book is printed on acid-free paper

1

Earl Collingwood slipped the gold ring off his finger and gave it to his son and heir, who was about to join Wellington's army fighting Napoleon.

'I want you to take my signet ring with you, Charles. It's an old family ring — a talisman — so it will protect you.'

Touched that his father had given him his precious jewelled ring with the family crest on the seal, thirty-year-old Viscount Charles Chard took the ring from his austere father, promising to look after it and return it to him after the battle.

Charles, a fortunate young man, had enjoyed inherited wealth all his life and was not keen to have his easy way of living interrupted. Yet he knew his dictatorial father was right when he'd told him it was about time he did something worthwhile.

It was not that Charlie was callous or selfish; hitherto he had simply neither necessity or opportunity to work, or to achieve something useful. Now he felt he should become a man worthy of his good fortune, earn respect, and be capable of taking his father's place when the time came. So he had taken the decision to leave his comfortable home behind and answer the call for men to defend England by enlisting in the army.

★ ★ ★

Months later, when people rejoiced to hear of Napoleon's defeat, Viscount Charles Chard lay writhing in pain among the slaughtered after the Battle of Waterloo.

After delivering a message for the Duke of Wellington, enemy soldiers had shot his horse, closed in around him and used their rifle butts to batter his prone body. The bullet meant to kill him had somehow missed his heart when they left him for dead.

Lying in the mire, in so much pain, Charlie wished each breath he took would be his last. He regretted that his parents would mourn their only son, and that he had no time now to fulfil their wish for him to marry and produce an heir.

Alas too, for the precious signet ring he'd been given by his father. As rescuers helped survivors off the battlefield and scavengers searched the injured for valuables, someone had stolen it.

Some time later, Charlie was saved by some kind French peasants who took him in and tended his wounds until he had recovered sufficiently to be brought back to England.

* * *

As Charlie lay on his sick bed, slowly healing, the Earl of Collingwood was loath to question his son about his missing signet ring.

When Charlie was well enough to be

3

able to stand and leave his room, although still feeling groggy, he faced his lordly father in the library of his grand mansion.

The normally distant Earl beamed as he said, 'Your mama and I were told by the Duke of Wellington that you acted bravely under fire. We are proud of you.' Then his father's smile vanished as he went on, 'I cannot blame you for the circumstances that led to my signet ring being stolen. Nevertheless, now I wish you to go and find it and return it to my possession.'

Charlie gulped, as his weakened leg pained him. His jacket, waistcoat and pantaloons hung loosely on his well-formed but now shrunken body after his illness.

'I intend to, Papa,' he said firmly, wishing he felt stronger.

His father noted his son's discomfort, but went on to explain why it was necessary for Charlie to locate his ring promptly, and return it to him.

'My bank has notified me to say that

the seal on my ring is being used as my signature. It is akin to me signing my name on paper debts . . . '

Horrified to think that anyone would use his father's stolen ring seal like a cheque book, Charlie frowned.

The earl's lips tightened. 'Alas, I shall soon be bankrupt if this fraud continues.'

An aggrieved sigh escaped Charlie's lips. What an impossible task he was being given when he was still unwell! He looked aghast at his father. Much as he longed to start on the quest to find his father's ring, Charlie was sure it was probably somewhere abroad, and he realised looking for it would be like looking for a needle in a haystack.

His mind in a whirl, Charlie replied, 'Papa, I promise I shall do my utmost to find your ring, even if I should die in the attempt!'

The earl raised his voice, saying, 'You will surely not be killed searching for a ring! You have sufficient wit, resourcefulness and skill. Wellington informed me you executed any order you were given.'

Pleased to hear his father was so confident in him, Charlie's smile temporarily lit up his grim expression, yet he feared he had been tasked with a hopeless errand. Turning to leave the library immediately, as if anxious to get started on his quest, his father called after him, 'And while you are about it, get married! You're already nearing thirty years old and we need an heir.'

Charlie could understand the urgency for that request too, but he had no more idea how to fulfil the second requirement than the first. He closed the library door quickly, in case this father thought to issue him any further challenging tasks.

Flummoxed, Charlie took a deep breath. What should he do?

He resolved to call on his friend, Horatio Gallinston. Simply being able to discuss his problems might give him some idea of how he could proceed with his two momentous tasks.

Mr Horatio Gallinston was an old

school friend who lived nearby. Exceedingly handsome and wealthy, he had an agreeable nature, although none of the gritty determination to prove himself that Charlie possessed.

Still sore from his injuries, Charlie rode over to see Horatio, yet with little hope that his friend would be able to help him in any way.

However, when the young men were sitting at ease on the sunny terrace overlooking the extensive deer parkland, enjoying a glass of brandy, Horatio listened to Charlie's troubles — then he made a suggestion that surprised him.

'I am to visit my fiancée, Harriet Gibbon, tomorrow and you may like to come along. Her older sister, Amy, is looking for a husband.'

'How do you know that?'

Horatio looked a little shamefaced as he explained that he was originally engaged to Amy, but that her little sister had enchanted him more and he had broken his promise to marry her.

'Surely your change of heart puts the older sister in a difficult position?'

'It does, I regret to say. And me too, for although I am convinced I do love Harriet and she loves me, and our natures suit . . . well, I have the guilty feeling that Amy still loves me.'

'Has this older sister become bitter?'

Horatio shook his head. 'No. Amy accepted I had fallen for her sibling and she has shown no resentment — even if she feels it — but I know Amy's prospects are not good. After her father Baron Gibbon died, her mother, Lady Gibbon, took charge of their estate as they have no son, and their affairs are going downhill. So I feel a responsibility to help Amy to find a husband who will at least give her an interesting life, away from the stifling home where she is trapped as companion to her ailing mother.'

'Ah!' said Charlie, whose mama suffered multiple illnesses, and would surely not make a young lady companion happy either. 'So, you think I may be suitable to be her husband?'

'Yes, Charlie, I think you may be. But only you can decide that when you meet her.'

Charlie swirled the golden liquid in his glass and sipped. 'Well, I suppose I shall have to make the effort to meet some eligible ladies so I may as well start with Miss Amy Gibbon.'

Both men looked at each other and grinned.

Horatio said, 'Very good, Charlie, we shall set off for Plate Hall early tomorrow, to be there in the afternoon. This late summer weather is good, so we can ride there slowly so as not to give your injured leg too much discomfort.'

* * *

Next day, during their leisurely ride along the countryside tracks, on their way to Plate Hall, with the leaves on the trees starting to turn red and gold and falling like confetti on the ground, the discussion turned to Charlie's other dilemma.

'I have been thinking about how I may set about searching for my father's ring,' Charlie explained. 'I know for certain that it is being used illegally, so someone must have it. Another thing I know is that the debts being mounted up come from somewhere in France because of the way the debts of honour are being written.'

Horatio nodded encouragingly, allowing Charlie to continue thinking aloud.

'Since Napoleon was defeated, an Army of Occupation has remained in northern Europe — although most officers and their men were sent home when the war ended. After the great Revolution in France, Napoleon began to make some improvements, but before long he had begun fighting again. His defeat has left the French much occupied with trying to reorganise themselves. It will take time, especially in some of the rural battlefield lands after the wars. Ex-soldiers, as well as the local people, have to survive and adjust their lives too.'

Horatio exclaimed, 'It sounds as

though that part of France is just the place one should avoid!'

Charlie agreed, but told his friend that was where he would have to go if he wished to find his father's ring.

'Rather you than me!' Horatio laughed.

'Well, yes.' Charlie had to agree. 'But you are not in my position. You lack a domineering father and an earldom to inherit. Your conscience is clear — mine, sadly, is not so.'

Horatio pressed his lips together, not wishing to annoy Charlie by pointing out that he too had an estate to manage — and was soon to be married and would have a family to look after. However, he recognised that Charlie's responsibilities and problems were far greater. They plodded along on their mounts, not speaking for a while.

Charlie broke the silence by saying, 'I remember I had an excellent army scout who, if I am able to find him, may be able to assist me in my search.'

He continued to plan how he might

contact this former army scout and hire him to track down his father's valuable ring.

With his mind primarily on his need to locate the scout, Tom Brown, Charlie rode on to meet his prospective bride. He felt buoyed up, as he saw for the first time a slight glimmer of hope ahead that both of his goals might yet be achieved.

Not that Charlie relished the coming meeting with the eligible woman — and even worse, having to make an offer to a woman he hadn't even met, knowing she was a rejected bride!

Charlie had never been popular with the young society ladies because he had never put himself out to be. His previous encounters with women had been nothing more than youthful passion, as no woman had ever made him feel in any way in love with her.

He fully accepted the fact that he needed an heir, but had managed to put off having to do anything about it — until now.

Today he had to rectify the situation, and with Horatio having confided that Amy Gibbon was at one time his sweetheart, it indicated that if she had been considered suitable for his friend, then she must also be suitable for him, which would save him a deal of trouble finding out about her.

She would, he hoped, be obliging, look presentable and be willing to accept his offer — in fact, he mused, as an older woman, she might be only too happy to marry money and receive a title.

Once quickly married, he could hop off abroad to find that damned ring! He might even enjoy the chase. Already, earlier that morning, he had sent a message to the Commander of the Occupation Forces in northern Europe, asking for his assistance in contacting Tom Brown. Tom would, he surmised, be glad of a job now that the army was being disbanded.

Tom and Charlie were as different as chalk and cheese. Charles Chard, from the nobility and an educated gentleman, had been thrown into army life and would have been eaten alive had not Tom Brown, an experienced soldier, stepped up to take care of him.

Charlie had intended to get in touch with Tom anyway, to thank him for his very necessary care and protection during his short time in the army when he was a raw recruit — even though Charlie had swiftly adapted to army life. His natural abilities and common sense were soon recognised by his fellow soldiers and he was promoted rapidly to the rank of captain.

Also, Charlie did not know — but he had the notion — that it may have been Tom who had found him lying injured on the battlefield and had arranged for him to be taken to the farmer's cottage to be nursed.

If that was indeed the case, then he felt he owed Tom some reward for saving his life.

2

'Money, money, money! Is that all you can ever talk about, Harriet?'

Miss Amy Gibbon felt instantly ashamed after saying those sharp words to her young sister. However, her outburst came after a warm September afternoon out in the grounds of Plate Hall, trying to pass the time by playing a game of croquet and now bowling hoops.

Eighteen-year-old Harriet Gibbon slammed her hoop and stick down on the leaf-strewn grass in a fit of temper, and stamped on them.

'Tell me, what is more important than money?' she cried out. 'If we had some money we could be out shopping in town trying on the prettiest bonnets instead of playing this silly game! You should know how necessary it is to have money, Amy. You have to wear my old clothes because Mama cannot afford new ones for both of us.'

Amy flinched as her sister scolded, because her words had truth as well as a touch of crowing in them.

Since the death of their father, Baron Gibbon, their mama was in charge of managing their finances, but she proved to have little aptitude for the task and now economies were urgently necessary. Consequently, Amy was regarded as having already had her expensive coming out, and not found a husband — therefore it was only fair to give her young sister Harriet her chance to shine in society.

Harriet went on in a tone of triumph, 'After all, I have to be well dressed because I am to marry a rich man and you are not.'

Although stabbed by the painful truth of what she said, Amy did not blame her young sister for having all the luck. At the age of twenty-five, Amy was old and wise enough to accept what life threw at her. Besides, she wanted happiness for her little sister — as well as for herself.

So it was with humility that she replied, 'I am not golden-haired and dainty like you, Harriet. I know very well that my looks do me no credit. Yet I seek only a comfortable future. Whether I am rich or poor, it will matter little to me.'

'Oh yes, it will! You wait until you have to beg in the streets!'

Amy bristled.

'There is a difference between being destitute and not having every single thing that you want.'

'Do not preach to me! I have my marriage lined up while you are on your last gasps for a husband of any kind!'

That was blatantly cruel of Harriet to remind her older sister of her predicament, and to hint at her unattractiveness. Amy knew too well that her chance of getting away from her endlessly tedious everyday chores were gone. No balls, dances or opportunities to meet interesting people that would break the monotony of life lay ahead for her. She did not need to be reminded of her dull future. A full-time housekeeper and companion for her mother was to be her lot. Day in, day out, marooned on the crumbling estate — each day was destined to be exactly the same for her.

Nevertheless, Amy reckoned her situation could be a good deal worse. She was determined to enjoy the simple things in life — and she did so as to the utmost of her ability.

Amy was not plain; she was simply not a beauty like her little sister. On the other hand, her nature was not so biddable as most eligible young men seemed to like their brides to be, although she was sensible and honest.

Still, facts had to be faced, she thought, and being volatile or vindictive was not in her character, so she resolved to allow Harriet's goading to float by her.

However, when Harriet saw the hurt on her older sister's face she was struck with remorse and immediately ran to embrace her.

'Oh, Amy, I'm so sorry to be ill-tempered this afternoon! I've been unkind to you. I couldn't have a sweeter sister — one who deserves the best of everything.'

Amy knew Harriet was contrite and she must put the painful episode behind her and forget it.

However, keeping her younger sibling entertained was no easy task. Young Harriet had a different character from herself. Harriet possessed little patience and was bored waiting for her betrothed, who was due for dinner that evening. Croquet with only two players, and now bowling hoops, were forms of outdoor exercise that were not so much fun as they had been when they were children. Still, either was preferable to moping indoors, where reading, embroidery and card games did not interest Harriet either.

Unfortunately, lack of family money was only part of the suffering that afflicted Amy. What Harriet did not know was that the man she was about to marry, Lord Horatio Gallinston, had been loved by Amy too. In fact, Amy had been practically engaged to Horatio before Harriet had noticed her sister's gentleman caller and decided she wanted him for herself. Her attractive, bubbly little sister had soon charmed him into a promise of marriage.

Hurt and humiliated, Amy knew that if Horatio had chosen her sister, so be it. She determined that she would never marry anyone else, because her heart would always belong to Horatio Gallinston.

Amy had to conceal her grief — she did not wish to spend her life moping. Neither did she wish to say anything that might bring a permanent friction between them, so she pressed her lips tightly together and struck her croquet stick savagely against her hoop, sending it spinning across the lawn and over the swirling leaves onto the drive, in front of the manor house.

Then she watched in horror as her hoop spun towards two riders who had come through the hall gates and were approaching the house.

Hands over her mouth, Amy watched fearfully.

'Whoa!'

The clip-clop of hooves became frantic leaps and whinnies from two startled horses, seeing the wobbly hoop advancing towards them. Fortunately, both riders were competent and soon quieted their prancing beasts, as the hoop wheeled by them and, after losing speed, fell over on the drive.

Dear me, I nearly caused an accident!

Amy chided her temper, which had nearly unseated the visitors and clearly earned her some unsavoury language from the men! She was glad to be far enough away not to hear properly.

'It's Horatio!'

Harriet's triumphant cry was followed by a quick flit across the lawn towards the riders, leaving Amy with a flushed face — and her heart torn in two, desperate to see the man she loved, but knowing that Horatio, Viscount

Gallinston, was not her man to claim any more.

Amy busied herself by collecting Harriet's abandoned hoop and stick, allowing time for her to stroll to meet the visitors, who had tethered their horses by the front door and were being greeted by Harriet.

Horatio's handsome looks, together with his wide smile as he jumped off his horse, made Amy envious as he ran to put his arm around Harriet. It sent a clear message: he had chosen her sister. He had never been so familiar with *her*.

She turned her attention to the second rider who dismounted gingerly, as if stiff — or was his leg injured? Amy stood still, her attention captured by the tall, grim-looking gentleman.

He was darkly dressed, like a vicar, yet quality showed in his country clothes. He stood viewing the grand but somewhat dilapidated Plate Hall, examining it — was that with an air of disdain? Or was it that he did not wish to impose his presence or embarrass the embracing young couple?

'Ah, Amy,' Horatio called to her as she approached. 'I've brought my friend, Charles, for you to inspect.'

Amy came closer and gave a polite curtsy to the stranger as she fumbled, trying not to drop the sticks and hoops.

The tall gentleman turned his attention to Amy, looking her over as though she was a horse for sale at Tattershall's horse fair.

Who is making the inspection? she wondered, nevertheless giving him a welcoming smile, which he acknowledged with a bow.

Admiring the cloth and cut of his suit and his highly polished boots, Amy felt it was a pity she was wearing the repaired dress that was probably the worst one in her meagre wardrobe. She hoped the stitching on the large tear in the front didn't show. She looked up at a weather-beaten, strong male face with shock — he was undoubtedly a handsome fellow, although not friendly-looking.

Who was this man? She felt sure he

was far from a nobody; he had presence, and Amy found herself unable to take her eyes off him.

'Let me collect the hoop you sent to down us,' he said, and while she watched mesmerised, he strode with a slight limp to pick up the other hoop. He ignored the young lovers when he came back. 'Hand me the rest,' he almost barked at Amy, as though talking to a servant, taking the rest of the games equipment from her hands. His voice was deep, commanding, and Amy felt she had no option but to obey him.

In the meantime, Harriet and Horatio, arm in arm, had entered the house, leaving Amy to entertain the other gentleman.

Amy could not help admiring the visitor. Unlike Horatio, his thoughtful and solemn air showed maturity. His quality attire enhanced his well-formed body, his bearing that of a soldier. She wanted to be properly introduced, so she asked, 'May I know your name, sir?'

Surprise registered on his face, as if

she'd insulted him. 'Won't Charles do?'

Amy smothered a smile as she dared to look up at his steely eyes. She had nothing to lose by being bold with him. After all, she was no longer a green girl, schooled by her mama to show her willingness to please men. It wasn't necessary for her to curb her curiosity. Horatio had told her Charles had been brought for her to inspect and she felt free to do just that.

'Is that all I am allowed to know, sir? Just Charles? I'm sure a gentleman like yourself would have been christened with a string of names — and your family name of course to be added to the list!'

He cracked his riding whip on his leather boots, clearly a little put out by her frankness.

'You are an inquisitive young lady, and — '

'Not so young, sir!' Amy corrected him brazenly. 'As my sister reminded me only just this afternoon, I'm on my last prayers.'

He frowned as he looked her over again, and then gave a hint of a smile.

So there is some life in the iceberg! she thought — but he remained silent.

She reverted to a more polite manner.

'Am I to understand that you prefer not to talk about yourself, sir?'

'You understand correctly.'

Amy gave a sigh but the suppressed smile on her lips betrayed the fact that she found his hauteur amusing.

'Well then, let us hope you are able to discuss other things.'

What made Amy so straightforward, so forthcoming with a complete stranger? She did not understand her own behaviour! Yet it was more than that — she had felt an enormous affinity to him. Almost as though, immediately on close inspection, she had found an extraordinary attraction towards him.

Surely not! Her heart was tied elsewhere with her sister's man, her eyes even now gazing towards the Hall to where Horatio had gone inside with Harriet, her hand on his arm.

Charles gave a cough to attract her attention.

'So, you consider yourself on the shelf, Miss Gibbon? Surely not! Although I would say you are certainly a well matured young lady.'

Amy pinked as she smiled ruefully. By calling her Miss Gibbon, it was clear he knew she was the elder sister. He had obviously already been told she was a rejected lady, who had not managed to obtain a husband during her coming-out years.

However, as Amy was not obliged to simper like a teenage girl, she felt her older age gave her the advantage of treating him as she might an equal, like a brother or a cousin.

'And what else has Horatio been telling you about me?' She raised an eyebrow — a charming quirk she had that went with her mysterious, intelligent smile.

*   *   *

Charlie almost gasped upon seeing Amy's lively expression. He had been told to expect a dowdy older sister who might be suitable as a bride for him since he badly needed an heir. But this not-so-young filly he considered would not only be suitable, she intrigued him. Although he sensed she might lead him a merry dance!

After years in the army, he had forgotten how enchanting well-brought up ladies could be — indeed, how challenging!

Some inner sense told him he liked her as he observed her lively eyes that shone like sapphires in the sunlight. Her figure was good too, despite her torn dress that she was endeavouring to hide. His parents could not object to her pedigree, so it was all decided in his mind — that very minute — that his marriage was arranged! And if he could decide so quickly and easily, so could she!

It was such a relief to have it settled.

He never would have dreamed that, after getting off the boat at Dover several weeks ago, and going home as an invalid, one major worry about his future might evaporate so quickly.

His parents would be pleased. His mama, regardless of the desire a son might have to have his own home and let his wife choose the baby things, would soon be preparing the nursery suite — repainting, choosing new wallpaper, getting the servants to fetch the cradle down from the attic, and of course, visiting to the shops for materials to make baby clothes . . .

★ ★ ★

If Amy had known what was going on in Charlie's mind, she would have laughed.

Nothing was further from her thoughts than the idea that she had been selected as his future bride. Although she did think that Charles promised to be an interesting guest, which was a rarity at Plate Hall. She looked forward to enjoying his company, perhaps drawing him out a little.

Charles had the good manners not to hurt her further by examining her ragged dress and cast his eyes down, rubbing the gravel with his booted toe. 'So, let me try and remember what I was told about you . . . '

'Oh, please do not, sir!' Amy was afraid the remarks her future brother-in-law had made about her might not be entirely flattering, since many may have come originally from her sister. 'I am sure you will soon form your own opinion of me — as I will of you.'

Struck by her candour, Charles almost laughed. It was a rare occurrence to find such lack of guile in a woman, to be able to talk to her in an honest way, with the freedom to be able to show his true nature.

It might surprise her to know that although he could be blunt, he had no intention of deceiving her, of ever hurting her. He had never made a habit of charming ladies, and he did not intend to beguile her. He would explain that their marriage would be a marriage of convenience because he needed an heir, and he would promise to treat her with respect.

'Sir, will you come in for a dish of tea after your long ride?'

Charles was keen to accompany his chosen bride into the house. For him it was like the curtain going up on a stage at the theatre; his interest was aroused and he wished to see how the play would proceed.

★   ★   ★

'Lead the way,' he said, indicating that she should go first.

Amy was acutely aware of her well-worn patched muslin, mended shoes, and hair that had not received the attention of a maid that morning, as they moved towards the front door.

However, she realised a man of his ilk would have already summed up her somewhat slovenly appearance and she could not pretend she was a servant because he knew she was not. The only hope she had, as she felt like a child caught with her hand in the sugar lump bowl, was to brazen it out. After all, he was only a friend of Horatio, and Amy would probably rarely see him again — possibly never, after Harriet's wedding.

'Leave the playthings by the front door,' she said. 'Thank you for carrying them for me, sir.'

He not only placed the hoops and sticks against the wall by the front door, he stepped ahead and opened the door for her.

That courtesy hurt Amy. Although it was correct, it only emphasised to her that he thought of her as a lady, although in poor circumstances. Perhaps he was amusing himself by treating her as though she had status when he knew she had none?

Yet, she felt he was naturally a gentleman, trained from childhood to show courtesy to a lady, even one of no consequence.

Stepping into the hall, she cast aside

her self-pity, as was her way, saying, 'I expect Mama will receive you in the drawing room. She usually takes tea there at this time in the afternoon.'

She was about to move to the drawing room when a shaggy-haired black and white sheep dog came bounding towards her with joyous barks and attempted to jump up and lick her.

'Sit down!' Charles's loud order almost shook the house.

The dog sat, its soulful eyes looking up anxiously up at the newcomer.

'I do beg your pardon, sir. My dog, Skippy, has not yet been fed,' Amy explained. 'He has been out with the herdsman rounding up the cows for milking.'

'No excuse for an unruly dog. I cannot abide bad manners in dogs. Or people.'

Amy felt as if she had been slapped, and she took an instant dislike to his voice of authority. He obviously expected high standards from everyone, including animals.

'I'm sure you like civility, as we all do, but my dog is a farm dog and has not been taught to bow,' she retorted, with a quirk on her lips.

'He can learn.'

Amy ignored the rebuke and patted Skippy's head fondly.

'I shall put it on my list of things to be done, sir. Now if you care to come this way we will join the others and you can partake of a dish of tea.'

As his riding boots sounded firmly behind her on the way to the drawing-room, Amy wondered if the tea and cakes would be anything like the high standard he might expect. Biddy, their cook, was not skilled at confectionery. Amy just hoped the tea cups had been properly washed and the tea strong enough for the men.

Skippy wagged his tail, having accepted the visitor's reprimand as he looked up at Charles as though he'd met his match, and docilely followed them into the grandest room in the house. Farm dog he might be, but he was Amy's pet too and was allowed the freedom of the house.

Voices inside told them that Lady Gibbon and her daughter, Harriet, were already busy entertaining Mr Horatio Gallinston.

Entering the spacious room, with its oak panelling and soft carpeting, Amy could not keep her eyes from fixing upon the man she still loved. Horatio was seated close to Harriet on the sofa, talking to Lady Gibbon, their mama. Horatio had such a well-formed, kind face . . . and he should have been *her* husband.

While Amy was helping the maid bring in the tea tray, formal introductions were made, and Lady Gibbon looked over Lord Charles with the help of her lorgnette. She remarked, 'I believe I was at school with your mama in Cheltenham.'

Charles enquired politely if she corresponded with his mama, but Lady Gibbon was too excited even to answer as her attention was given totally to the young couple on the sofa near her.

Amy did not miss the slight her mother had given Charles by not replying to his question, and immediately offered him a chair. Then she went to fetch him a cup of tea and a currant bun that looked somewhat over-cooked and she hoped he would refuse to eat. However he accepted everything offered with a nod and ate the cake as if he was hungry, ignoring the dog's eyes requesting to be fed some of it.

Seeing her mother continuing to ignore her guest, Amy helped herself to tea and sat in a chair beside Charles, hoping to entertain him by making polite conversation.

'I do hope your mama is well?' she asked, taking a sip of tea.

'She is not, Miss Gibbon. She suffers from many ladies' ailments . . . frequent fainting, vapours, nerves — as well as unfulfilled hopes and dreaded fears.'

With difficulty she hid her amusement at hearing the lengthy list, which indicated to her that the matron was in a sorry state.

'I am sorry for it,' she said, thinking he might be teasing her, 'but is not that list of ailments suffered by both male and female?'

'My mama excels at them, Miss Gibbon.'

Amy almost choked on her tea and hastily put her cup down. Perhaps he was not joking and his mother had a deal of suffering to endure?

'I am sorry to hear it,' she said again, summoning genuine sympathy, thinking the lady must be a permanent invalid.

'You were not to know. She will no doubt be always complaining, but parents do not last forever.'

To gloss over the somewhat callous remark, Amy added with a heartfelt sigh, 'I know — my papa is in heaven.'

'Is he, now?'

This conversation was difficult, but Amy persevered. 'Your papa is well, I trust?'

'Miss Gibbon, my father is never unwell.'

She felt like saying, *well thank*

goodness for that! but asked instead, 'As you are also, I trust?'

'Do I look unwell?'

Amy gave a slight shiver as she shook her head. He was about as desirable physically as a man could be, but she suspected he knew that. She looked up at the decorative plasterwork on the ceiling trying to compose a suitable answer.

'Try looking at me, Miss Gibbon. There's nothing as good as observation. Do I look as though I was near to death a few months ago?'

Reluctantly she turned her eyes towards him. She liked what she saw, but was aware of those intelligent eyes reading her like a book — almost devouring her! She had already detected his slight limp and his complexion, although healthy, had a few scars to show he had been in a battle.

His lips tantalised her . . . what would it be like to be kissed by him? She felt her colour rising uncomfortably.

At this point Horatio saved her by standing up and crossing the room to them.

'Yes indeed, Amy, Captain Charles Chard was badly injured and left for dead on the battlefield at Waterloo until he was found and nursed back to health.'

For an uncharitable moment Amy thought it a pity the captain was not left there, as he was plaguing her to death!

Yet he did not seem in the least put out by Horatio's reference to his past misfortune and he replied to his friend, 'I am concerned only with my future now — as Miss Gibbon should be thinking of her future, too.'

3

Draining his tea cup, Charles put it down on a nearby table and stood to whisper in Horatio's ear, 'I would appreciate the opportunity to have a private conversation with Lady Gibbon.'

Horatio looked shocked and turned Charles's shoulder away from Amy, so he could question him confidentially.

Amy's ears pricked as she was just able to detect Horatio asking with an astonished voice, 'Now? Are you sure, Charlie? So soon after your first meeting?'

'Certainly. I think the older sister should be married first,' Charles whispered back.

Amy frowned. She should not have been listening, she supposed, and yet it sounded as though this arrogant guest was going to ask her mother if he could propose to her!

She must have misunderstood. They'd only just met. Yet whatever was on his mind intrigued her.

Immediately she stood saying, 'The orchids are doing very well this year, Charles. Would you care to view the orchid house?'

Charles eyed her and replied, 'Lead the way, Miss Gibbon.'

Horatio was left open-mouthed as Amy swept out of the room towards the conservatory and orchid house. With a bow to the occupants of the room, Charles followed her.

As she walked by each flowering plant, Amy gave the botanical name to it. The earthy smells of the plants, as well as the rich array of the exotic flowers, were breathtaking.

She remembered Charles's injured leg, so she made for a garden chair and indicated that he sat on it, saying, 'Take your ease, sir. Rest as a wounded warrior should.'

'I am not an invalid, Miss Gibbon. I intend to remain on my feet.'

'As you wish sir, but I shall sit,' which she promptly did.

Having arranged her dress as best she could to avoid the tear showing, she said, 'Now tell me which of these flowers do you like best?'

'I have not come here to discuss orchids.'

Amy smiled. 'No, indeed. You do not strike me as a gentleman like my father, who was an orchid collector. Tell me what you enjoy ... horse racing, perhaps? Or card playing?'

'It is not my interests that I wish to speak to you of.'

'Of what, then?'

'Marriage.'

Amy gave a short laugh. 'I know nothing of the state. I am a spinster, and after my sister is married I intend to look after my mother, but also to pursue my life in my own way, as well as I am able to.'

He cleared his throat. 'I wish to discuss the time before your sister is married, not after.'

Her eyebrow rose with the corners of her lips.

'Oh, indeed! Well, you have not much time, sir, as I believe the nuptials are being discussed at this very moment. Harriet's autumn wedding is planned, and I shall be very busy helping the maids to prepare her trousseau, the flowers in the church, and that sort of thing.'

'And what if you were to be married before that event, Miss Gibbon?'

She turned her head to look at her father's plants and sighed rather sadly as she thought of Horatio and how it would have been if she could have been the bride instead of her sister.

She knew Charles was looking intently at her and she should comment about his remark. He wouldn't know how painful it was for her to think of an apt reply when her heart felt so heavy, that she was fighting the need to hide her disappointment in love.

'I think that is impossible.'

'Why?'

'Because . . . '

Amy felt a lump in her throat and her eyes began to fill with tears. How embarrassing to show the emotion she felt about Horatio and had been trying so hard to hide.

'Tell me, what is upsetting you?' he said softly, sitting down next to her — very close.

The situation was becoming unbearable and she wanted to sweep away from him, but he took one of her hands firmly and she had not the strength to release it — or perhaps she did not truly wish to. No one had been sympathetic about her position before, and his manner was kindly.

She took a deep breath and said, 'Sir . . . I shall never marry.'

'And why is that?'

'Because . . . because I love someone whom I cannot marry.'

Shocked that she had confessed her well-kept secret — and to a man she had only just met — she felt vulnerable. She simply could not understand what had come over her.

His large hand stilled her fidgety fingers in her lap. Quietly he asked, 'Horatio, you mean?'

Amazed he'd guessed the truth, Amy nodded miserably. She'd responded to his deeply authoritative voice just as her dog had earlier. Something about his experience with life and ability to command sounded in his question.

'Oh, please, you must not tell Horatio or Harriet! Or anyone!' she shrieked. 'I don't know why I told you. I feel I must die of shame!'

'No need for you to be embarrassed, Miss Gibbon. First loves are not necessarily our lifetime lasting love. Marriage is an arrangement between two consenting adults, for various reasons. But if one changes their mind and decides to marry another — it can happen, especially in a long engagement — then the one who is left is free to choose again. There is no shame in that. Horatio has chosen another lady so you are now free. And I should like to marry you.'

Her heart was thumping violently.

'No, you do not. You feel sorry for me.'

He lifted her hands and kissed the back of them. Ignoring her protest, he took a long breath and said in his attractively deep voice, 'I think you and I will suit each other very well. My parents desire an heir before I am much older — they were worried when I was almost killed at Waterloo.'

Now she understood his need to marry — he was after any eligible female to provide an heir! But why was he asking her? It was humiliating to think that she was simply available. He did not have to declare his love for her because it was not necessary. Although she found herself attracted to him — she couldn't deny it — love was not necessary on her side either.

Romantic love, she had been told, could be both blissful and at the same time painful, and her own experience, loving Horatio, had been so much of the time. But to marry without love was

. . . well, it was calculating . . . like being sold as a slave!

He placed a handkerchief in her hands so she could dab her tearful eyes. His proposal was way beyond her wildest dreams — but it was simply a marriage of convenience for him and his parents.

Yet a nagging voice asked whether the arrangement might just suit her too.

'So you came here believing I might be the kind of lady only too willing to accept you, and promptly, because Horatio said I was available?'

'Yes. Horatio told me of his earlier attachment to you, but that he now loves your sister, Harriet. She is the kind of young woman he desires to live with for the rest of his days. However, he is anxious for you to find a husband. Let me assure you that he has the greatest admiration for you and wants only the best for you.'

'A marriage of convenience does not sound like the best to me!'

He was silent for a moment before he

said slowly, 'Well, that is for you to decide. If you feel you can tolerate me as your husband, and whether you feel you can trust me to give you a pleasant home?'

Amy turned to look straight into his eyes, and blinked, but she found no arrogance there.

It seemed he was having a hard time explaining his need to marry — and to convince her of it. She listened while he continued, 'I must admit I have not led a blameless life so far. Some might call me a rake, although I would protest. It is simply that I have never met a woman I have wished to marry. Indeed, I had to be almost killed before I accepted it was my duty to marry. However, now that I have met you, Amy, I have the chance to rectify the situation, because I do genuinely feel that we could deal well together.'

She said nothing but looked up and studied his noble profile. He was staring at his boot, as if he hated having to admit his need for a wife. For a moment she felt sorry for him! What had brought this gentleman to have to scrape the bottom of the barrel for a wife? He struck her as a wealthy nobleman, and older sons were always worried about producing an heir, so his need was genuine. But what had he been doing with his youth? Why had he not found a suitable bride before he had come to this humiliation of having to ask an older girl in the leftover basket?

She shifted a little away from him saying, 'If I say, no thank you, will you be off to seek another suitable lady left on the shelf?'

'No,' he countered firmly, 'I have now found the lady I want. I just have to persuade her that I am the man she wants.'

She waited for him to say more, but he seemed to be waiting for her to speak as the minutes went by.

Eventually she snapped, 'If I am indeed the lady you have found who you think will suit you so well, then sir, please say so.'

He gave a sudden laugh. 'You are!'

'That is utter folly! We have only just met. How can you possibly know if I might suit you?'

He turned to face her. He was not smiling.

'I just know,' he said. 'Call it intuition.'

She blushed as his gaze was intense. She would have preferred he had said he would love her, but how could he? And she would not have believed him anyway.

'So, Charles, to put it in another way, you wish me to produce a child for you, as promptly as possible?'

Did he look a trifle embarrassed? As well he should be!

'Is that not the idea of marriage? I need an eligible heir and you need a husband. There is nothing wrong with that, Miss Gibbon. Unless you are thinking of becoming a nun?'

'I think they would not have me in a convent!'

He caught her eye and they both smiled.

'Do you prefer to live here with your mama? I think you are the kind of woman who would find it extremely dull. I should think your mama is not very sharp with cards.'

That was true; her mother was nowhere near as intelligent as she was. Amy realised he had already observed that. She could do with respite from the rut she was in and saw no prospect of getting away from it — except now, in an unexpected proposal of instant marriage!

She ought to take his offer seriously, and be as forthright about it as he had been.

She swallowed and said, 'What do you offer me? A husband who is more interested in other women and is rarely at home?'

'My years of chasing women are over.'

She couldn't imagine that stony-faced man chasing anyone — surely that was why he was single, spurned by women, as he spurned them. He, like she, had a lot to learn about the opposite gender. An adventure was in store for her — *if* she were reckless enough to accept his offer.

She looked past him at her father's orchid conservatory. Her dear papa had had a harmless interest in collecting orchids. It was not a vice, and she should not wonder whether Charles had any vices, but she did. She had many things that interested her; interests she could pursue.

She asked, 'Then you would be out hunting, shooting or fishing. Or do you have some secret vice?'

'Why, Miss Gibbon! You are well informed about men's habits.'

She smiled. 'Papa permitted me to read his daily newspaper.'

He pursed his lips and she had a sudden longing for him to kiss her! That his muscular arms might encircle her and he might crush her to his broad chest!

He gave a little cough and brought her back to the moment.

'In point of fact, I do have a vitally important journey to make — a quest to fulfil.'

'May I know what it is? Is it part of our bargain that you will be jaunting off as soon as . . . ?'

A rosiness coloured her cheeks. She had thrown herself into telling him that she would be as ready to mate as a brood mare!

'No. My quest has nothing to do with my marriage, but it has to be dealt with immediately.'

'A mystery?'

He shook his head. 'It need not concern you. I hope to clear the matter up promptly, but I have to rely on help from a friend.'

'Horatio?'

'No,' he replied quickly, 'another man who was in the army with me.'

She examined his face more closely but soon realised he was not going to tell her what this mission was all about. She pressed her lips together.

'So all you want from me is a baby

son? And to not interfere with whatever it is you intend to run off and do?'

'No, no! Of course that is not *all*. I want a wife of consequence. A lady I can respect, who will run her household efficiently, and take her place in society — '

'While you run off to pursue your interests? And you refuse to tell me what they are?'

'Hmm . . . only for a while . . . '

He appeared to hesitate as though reluctant to betray a secret. Whatever it was, she could detect a vulnerability which melted her heart towards him. He might be a tough ex-soldier, a strict landowner, but he was not without emotional intelligence — he was showing her things he cared about deeply.

He said, 'Very well, I suppose it is only fair to tell you that I intend to go to France to find my father's signet ring that was stolen from me after the Battle of Waterloo.'

Her eyes glistened. 'You mean you wish to go on a treasure hunt?'

'Right first time, Miss Gibbon. But I am afraid it will be no game.'

'I would enjoy a trip to France.'

His lips tightened. 'I had not considered that you might want to step anywhere near danger.'

'Are we not friends with the French now?'

He smiled slightly. 'At present we have an Army of Occupation there. Some French people might resent us. Also you must realise that travel anywhere abroad is hazardous — gentlewomen especially can find it uncomfortable — and where I fear I may have to venture is very perilous. It is not a grand tour of the sights of the ancient world. Where I will have to go are places best avoided. I know not where my search may take me.'

Although he obviously wished to give her a grim picture of travelling abroad, it had the opposite effect on Amy, whose thirst for adventure exceeded even her desire for marriage.

'Would you take me to France if I

agreed to marry you? I long for travel,' she implored him. 'I have read about other countries and my closeted life has made me feel like a caged bird. For me it would be a dream come true to be able to see the wider world, to experience the sights and sounds of somewhere other than Plate Hall. Anywhere abroad would be like opening up a new life!'

He chuckled. 'Are you demanding a bargain?'

'I may as well get something I would like from the arrangement!'

He lowered his head to kiss her flushed cheek.

'I do believe you are indeed the kind of woman who would manage the inconveniences very well, and even enjoy the experiences. I would take the greatest care that you were not placed in any danger. However, I think we should wait until the situation in France is more settled. Then I promise I will take you on a jaunt.'

For the first time in many years,

excitement bubbled up inside Amy. That sounded a wonderful promise of an exciting adventure — much better than any she'd dreamed up on the dreary days at Plate Hall. However, there was a condition first that she had to be prepared to fulfil . . .

A leap into marriage!

She felt her face flush and her fingers lock together. She wanted to shout, *Don't be absurd!* His proposal was outrageous, coming out of the blue like a cannon being fired at her.

Yet she did wish to marry, to have a home of her own and children, rather than become the tired spinster she seemed destined to become. He would know as well as she that a conventional ritual, of courting a woman and agreeing to a settlement, would normally precede marriage and that might take months. For some reason he wished to discard those niceties that a marriageable girl might expect and was looking to find a woman prepared to marry at short notice.

Even so, she was attracted to him, even to being married without an engagement period, and she had to make the decision right now . . .

She swallowed and heard herself asking in an incredulous voice that hardly seemed like her own, 'Am I to understand that you came here today to ask for my hand?'

He looked slightly abashed. She felt pity for him, a war hero who'd needed a wife.

But did they not each need the other, if for different reasons? She smiled; a little humour was better than playing the part of a woman injured by having such a raw offer thrown at her.

Her lips twitched as she said, 'Charles, the manner of your proposal is shocking. However, I am tempted to take up your offer of an adventure abroad — which means I must marry you first?'

He chuckled. 'I think it would not your reputation no good if you did not! Besides, my heir must be born in wedlock.'

Amy's face coloured as she fingered the neckline of her dress. 'I cannot believe we are discussing such intimacies . . . '

'Well, we are. We have to say honestly what we think and want and intend to do. What other people might think of our arrangements is of no consequence. It is *our* lives we are planning — and unfortunately we must hurry over it.'

What a gamble! What a risk she would be taking if she agreed to his sudden, unexpected offer of marriage! However, was it not most girls' dream to marry? She knew she had always wanted to.

This man she was assessing was undoubtedly the kind of man she had always admired. He had the air of a commander, pleasing manners and a tall physique. His leg injury would not allow him to be a dancer, but what did that matter to her, who spent most assemblies now seated with the matrons at the side of the ballroom? She liked his features, his warm voice, the smell of him. She longed for the feel of his kiss on her lips . . .

Jolted by the sudden possible change in her circumstances, she tried to be sensible and consider the two main reasons that made her feel her outlook had already been changed.

One was that she knew in her heart that her yearning after Horatio was now over. The other reason was her judgement of Charles. She had to admit she liked him, felt flattered that he had made her an offer. But was it the right thing to do — to cast aside her worries about the absurd manner of his proposal and abandon her plans for spinsterhood? Should she allow this man, of whom she knew nothing, take her to goodness knows where and make love to her? Did she really want to step into this vast unknown?

Looking at him would not tell her what to do. She had studied his appearance and found she approved of it — but appearances could be deceptive. A good-looking, well-heeled gentleman could be as easily be a rogue as any rogue in irons in prison.

The more she tried to sort out her befuddled brain, the more clouded it became.

'Hello, you two!'

Harriet's running footsteps broke into their reverie. It would not have occurred to Harriet that she might be intruding upon a critical moment in her sister's life.

'Introduce me to Viscount Chard, then,' Harriet demanded, giving Charles a curtsy.

Viscount Chard? Amy blinked. So that was what Charles was hiding — his ancestry and his high status in society. Well, he certainly had not been trying to woo her with his title and wealth, and for that she was grateful.

Harriet continued, 'You should not be hogging our guest, Amy. I wish to learn all about him.'

Amy was used to being told off by her younger sister and said nothing, but Charles stood and looked down at the interfering girl, saying with the same commanding voice as he had spoken to the dog, 'Miss Harriet, your sister and I have important matters to discuss and we have not finished yet. Leave us alone, if you please.'

Amy almost laughed to see her sister being corrected! In addition, she could suddenly enjoy the prospect of the status she was being offered — as a Viscountess.

With a surprised and warning look at Amy, Harriet bobbed a curtsey and hurried away.

'Was I too hard on your sister?' Charles sat down beside Amy again — very near, so she could feel the warmth of his body — and took her hand.

'No — Harriet is a dear child but has need of a stricter chaperone than I. Horatio will make her a good husband, I am sure of that.'

'And what of us?'

Amy inhaled deeply and blushed.

'I expect Harriet has run off and told Mama about our assignation. So it will come as no surprise to her that we are . . . '

'Betrothed?'

Amy squeezed her eyes shut and felt she did not want to move away from him — or demand that he stop rubbing her hand with his thumb. It was as though she stood atop a high cliff trying to decide whether to jump, with someone who wished to take the same risk as she did.

Would she regret it forever if she refused him? This was a moment in her life she knew was vital for her future.

Having made up her mind, almost against her will, she murmured, 'Yes.' Then she repeated in a stronger voice, trying to remember what was the correct thing to say after accepting a proposal of marriage, 'Yes, I will marry you, Charles.'

His arm came around her as she felt herself drawn to him. His lips touched hers with such tenderness that she lost all sense, except for pleasure. The burning passion she remembered from years ago when Horatio had kissed her returned, but this time the fire blazed with a stronger intensity. Her response was instinctive as she lost the power to do anything but return his kiss, revealing her own sensual desire.

When he drew away from her his expression showed a kindness she had not expected, and she was content for him to kiss her hand.

'Shall we inform your mama?' he asked.

Knowing he was in a hurry to get the purpose of his visit over, she nodded.

As he offered her his arm, Amy's mind was in turmoil. How could she let herself be persuaded into the most important decision in her life in a matter of only half an hour?

The only answer that came to mind was that, for no reason she could think of, she had fallen in love with this powerful, wealthy nobleman, Charles, Viscount Chard. Just like that! It was madness!

She hoped she would not live to regret it.

4

Harriet had obviously told her mother and fiancé that she had been sent away from the conservatory where the couple were conversing. What she had also obviously told them was that she had noticed the goings-on between her sister and Lord Chard. Indeed the report had been graphic enough to make her mama and Horatio forget all about her forthcoming wedding, and to anticipate another.

Three pairs of eyes looked expectantly at Charles and Amy as they entered the drawing room arm-in-arm. Everyone looked at everyone else, wondering who was going to speak first.

Horatio rose suddenly and, taking Harriet's hand, almost pulled her to her feet. 'I think we should go and inspect the gift I have brought you, Harriet. It is in my saddle-bag.'

Harriet looked clearly in a quandary, wanting to hear what was going to be said by her sister and the visitor — but also anxious to have her gift.

Horatio knew of course, and was determined to start keeping his little bride in order. He bowed and gently ushered Harriet out of the drawing room with determination and instructions that they go to the stables, away from the house.

Amy approved of his masterly ruse to remove Harriet — and also seeing him begin to take charge of the sometimes wilful young lady.

When they had departed, Amy went over to sit beside her mother.

'I know this will surprise you, Mama . . . but I wish to marry Charles.'

It was bold, earth-shattering news for Lady Gibbon who had barely managed to cope with the death of her husband, and now *both* her daughters were planning to leave her.

She looked aghast and wailed, 'But neither you or I even know this aristocratic gentleman.'

Amy replied promptly to give her mother little time to consider what was taking place.

'That is why Charles came here today, Mama, so that you will get to know him. You are acquainted with his mother — you told us so. And Horatio knows him well, and . . . ' Amy considered very carefully what she intended to say, truly believing it had actually happened, although she could not understand how it could be. 'And I am in love with him.'

'Impossible!'

Amy waited for Charles to say something — but he did not. So she continued boldly, 'No, Mama, it is not impossible. It has happened. And although you may consider it absurd, I grant you, it is the truth. Further, Charles tells me he can obtain a special licence for us to marry within days so that all the preparations for Harriet's wedding will not have be altered.'

Lady Gibbon's mouth moved silently,

not deciding to smile, or have what Charles told her his own mother suffered, a bout of the vapours.

Amy tried to think where her smelling salts had been placed, but then Charles calmly took control of the situation, obviously used to dealing with his mother's nerves.

Amy marvelled at his skilled bedside manner to calm her. They were soon discussing many things — but the word *love* she did not hear mentioned. Her mother seemed more interested in practical matters, such as explaining Amy's lack of dowry.

Charles mentioned his parents, and was able to say he knew they would be delighted to hear about his engagement. Yes, the Earl of Chard and his lady were aware that he was to be married — although not to whom, of course, but he did not mention that.

Yes, he had a fortune, as well as a title. Yes, he would love and care for Amy, and she would be able to visit her mama regularly. No, he did not desire a grand wedding, and neither did Amy. They would be living in his houses — one in London, and one on a thriving country estate — and Lady Gibbon would always be welcome to visit them.

'And what about her wardrobe?' Lady Gibbon fired at her future son-in-law. 'I am sure you will have noticed Amy is in need of new muslins?'

Charles did not embarrass Amy by replying that he had noticed her poor state of dress. Nor did he allow Lady Gibbon to be embarrassed by it, as he knew her younger daughter needed all the money she had for her trousseau. He said he felt sure Amy would soon look as well attired as any lady of fashion when she had decided what she would like, as soon her allowance from him was made available to her.

'Naturally, Amy will need to restock her wardrobe, as her place in the fashionable world demands that a lady is well dressed and I will see to it that a lady of fashion is hired to advise her. However, in the short time before Amy is wed, can a sewing maid not provide her with some serviceable garments?'

'How many?'

'As many as she needs, madam. The bill can be sent to me.'

Hearing this, Amy flushed, thinking the whole arrangement of her wedding was going to be too embarrassing at times. But she supposed that she had best get used to it. At least Charles was evidently going to be a generous husband, anxious she should have what she needed — even before the marriage ceremony.

Relief made Lady Gibbon smile at Charles. She was not being made to feel she was expected to provide for her eldest daughter more than she was comfortably able to do so — and Harriet was not going to be put out.

Amy was filled with peace, seeing her mother so kindly treated, and knowing Charles was telling her no lies — as far as she knew.

He was bewitching her mother as he had her, not with his status and wealth, but with kindness and understanding of her widowed position in society. He did not allow her to think that she was to be cast aside, made to feel unimportant, or that she would lose her daughter completely. He was not bribing her with promises nor making excuses for whisking her away, but simply stating facts that were, from her point of view, totally of benefit to her.

What mama would not want her daughter married to a wealthy, high-status man? No mention was made of Amy being badly in need of a husband, nor that she was taking a risk with a man she hardly knew, nor that they wished to marry in haste.

Amy admired his thoughtfulness and only hoped it would extend to her . . .

*   *   *

Amy had a few days to ponder over Charles's character and sincerity, but

they were days packed with preparations for her marriage and going away.
She felt as though she were in a dream,
inhabiting an unknown world. In any
event, she soon would be!

Accepting a marriage of convenience
to a man she judged to be honest in
providing her with a comfortable life in
exchange for giving him an heir, she
looked forward to having many material
gains.

Fortunately, her mother and sister
showed her only kindness and fur-
nished her with essentials as best they
could. Amy was determined not to take
anything her mama or Harriet might
need, saying she would be able to buy
what she wanted when she knew more
about her new life.

'Charles will provide me with a
generous allowance, I am sure,' she told
them as an excuse not to take anything
that was not already hers. 'Until I know
my new circumstances I cannot say
what I might require.'

Amy could tell that would not satisfy

Harriet, nor any young bride, but her nuptials were not to herald a bridal feast but a plain marriage of convenience. However, she expected to walk into a life of luxuries, the best money could buy. She anticipated she would never be short of life's comforts — soon able to enjoy putting together a wardrobe of clothes she liked, made by the best dressmakers, shoe-makers and bonnet stylists.

For Amy it was a period of many emotions that kept rising and falling. At times she thought she may have lost her senses. She felt fearful of what might happen. She felt proud to be marrying a member of the nobility, then worried she would feel an outcast. Round and round in her mind, both good and bad thoughts bombarded her.

She was sorry the older servants would miss her and her ability to run the household, so she made sure they were able to rearrange their work to continue providing comfort for her mama. Having neither herself nor her sister to serve in the future would mean they would have less work, so it was not necessary for more staff to be hired.

Her mother had a few close friends in the neighbourhood to provide her with companionship so Amy did not feel she was abandoning her mama to a wretched old age. After all, it was accepted that daughters did marry and move out of their childhood home.

Skippy, the dog, she decided to take with her. He had been trained to herd sheep but when her father died and the Home Farm had been left neglected, Skippy was unwanted and Amy had taken care of him. Now she was fond of him and the thought of leaving him was unbearable. Lord Chard was bound to have a few dogs in his establishments, so she was confident he would not mind having another.

As the day set for her wedding came nearer, Amy had bouts of feeling almost panic-struck.

Then one evening, Harriet came into her room for a sisterly chat. Comparing their feelings, Amy discovered her young sister had very similar hopes and fears about her own coming marriage.

Sitting on her bed as they did, as though Amy was reading her young sister a bedtime story, they were able to declare their apprehension about the abrupt change in their lives. It was not the older sister giving advice or the younger sister asking for it. Their conversation was entirely about their new lives and their lack of knowledge about the intimacies of marriage, and being thrown into high society without the knowledge and skills they felt they were lacking.

It was comforting for them both to realise that they were marrying men they believed would not ill-treat them, and that their mama would never have agreed to part with them had she suspected they were not about to embark on good marriages.

The girls promised each other they would keep in touch, and that their sisterly love would last.

Perhaps, although her marriage to Lord Charles Chard was to be quick and for the convenience of everyone, including herself, it could be as successful as her sister's carefully and properly arranged marriage? Both young women hoped for that. And no doubt the men they would marry would be hoping for the same.

★　★　★

A few days later, in crisp early autumn weather, the quiet wedding ceremony between Amy and Lord Charles Chard was performed in the village church, with only family and friends present. Charles brought along a few friends of his own, and Horatio was best man.

The Earl of Collingwood and his lady attended their son's wedding ceremony. Their visit was brief, but enough for Amy to recognise that she did not dislike Charles's gruff, stately old father, or his frail wife — who was not unlike her own mother in character. Amy could well understand why they were keen for Charles to marry and have an heir, and they in turn did not seem displeased with their son's choice of bride.

The church blessing was given, the wedding band placed on Amy's finger, well-wishes were said, and embraces over.

Her mind in turmoil — but not distressed — Amy began her new life with a fluttering stomach as the carriage taking them to their honeymoon destination pulled away from everything she had known in her life.

As the carriage passed the signpost showing the direction to London, Amy began to wonder if she had made the right decision. Fear stabbed at her, thinking particularly of this coming night, when she knew so little of what to expect. She naïvely hoped that once with her husband might be sufficient for her to get with child.

She was not afraid — only apprehensive as any virgin bride would be, she reasoned.

Charles's manners were as a gentleman should be; his kisses were tender. She wished he would show some passion when he kissed her hands and lips — but how could he, if he did not feel he was in love with her?

* * *

They arrived at London as the daylight faded. The nights were drawing in, and a breeze reminded people as they walked outside to take their coats and muffs and to tie their hats on their heads securely.

Street lights gave Amy a glimpse of the enormous size of the metropolis. It staggered her. The number of people about, from tradesmen to the fashionably attired, and the many buildings from old architectural gems to newly constructed Regency edifices, suitably impressed the new Viscountess Chard.

Charles's town house was a fine, elegant building in the fashionable part of town. His servants were lined up ready to receive them, bowing and curtsying and politely welcoming her as though she was of the nobility — which she now was. They watched her anxiously. But after they had examined her and found a mature young lady was to be their new mistress, they soon relaxed. Amy, too, was relieved to sense she had been accepted as the new lady of the house.

A fresh-faced, fair-haired slip of a girl was introduced as her personal maid. Amy wished she was older — less attractive — and immediately wondered if she would be looking after the maid rather than the girl looking after her! But the girl's friendliness and enthusiasm to be helpful made Amy take to her.

Charles commented, 'My housekeeper heard that you have no personal maid, and at this late hour, one had to be hurriedly hired to serve you. She is my housekeeper's niece. I am sure you will be tolerant of her lack of training. If she proves to be unsatisfactory, you may wish to have another maid. There are many skilled ladies' maids for hire in London. She was only chosen for quick convenience.'

Amy was relieved her new maid was as ignorant of what a skilled lady's maid should do as she was! She was also pleased to hear from Charles that her aunt was a highly trained housekeeper.

'Her aunt, Bishop, has been my housekeeper here since I was a boy, and I hope you will find her housekeeping skills most satisfactory, as I do.'

Amy was thankful to meet the older servant, who appeared pleasant and capable. Amy felt sure she would not have recommended her niece unless she was certain the girl was trainable.

In the privacy of the bedroom, Amy smiled at her new maid. 'I do not wish to call you by your surname, although I know it is customary,' she told the girl. 'What is your first name?'

'Molly, ma'am,' replied the girl with a wide friendly smile.

'Molly, just as you need to learn your

trade, I too must learn about life in London.'

The girl looked her new mistress up and down. 'The first advice I offer, ma'am, is that your gown is more suitable for your mother than for you.'

Amy laughed. 'You are right, Molly. This is my mama's gown altered to fit me! My wardrobe is in need of replacement. Do you sew?'

Molly shook her head. 'No, but Mama does.'

'That's splendid.'

Indeed, it was marvellous to think that soon she could shop for the best dress materials in London and have them made to suit her. In fact everything Amy observed in the house and staff pleased her and calmed her racing heart. Yet she missed her family and the people she'd known all her life, surrounded as she was now by strangers.

It was only later that evening when she had been shown the house and garden, holding Charles's hand for comfort, that the terrifying prospect of him making love to her rose up to distress her already tired mind and body.

It was necessary to fulfil her part of the bargain of her marriage that she should become his wife physically, and that she was fortunate she wasn't appalled at the idea of physical union with him — just apprehensive.

Although they talked together amicably and she was interested in all he was telling her about London, she was not relaxed and only picked at her evening meal, seeing him relish his food. He appeared to have no concerns about their first night together.

The event however did not come about, because an urgent message delivered by horseback rider was given to her husband just before they were about to retire . . .

5

Reading the letter handed to him by his butler, Charles said apologetically, 'Amy, I regret to have to tell you that I must leave for the Continent immediately. My scout, Tom Brown, has sent me this message to say he has traced my signet ring, and unless I go now and claim it, it will probably disappear and I shall never locate it again. I must cross the Channel tonight.'

Amy noted the far-away look in his eyes. What was it about his ring that had the power to make him want to leave immediately — even on his wedding night?

'I understand.' She nodded, although she did not appreciate why he had to rush abroad on this very night. 'We will go and pack our travel bags immediately.'

'We?'

'Of course. We agreed I should accompany you abroad.'

He frowned. 'Did we?' He looked as though he was trying to remember. 'I mean . . . did I?'

Amused that he had forgotten, she smiled and nodded emphatically. 'Yes, you did.'

He looked down at her and cleared his throat.

'Amy, it is not an educational tour of Europe that I am about to undertake, nor a joy ride for a lady. Many difficulties or mishaps might occur. It may take weeks for me to track down who has my ring — and even then, whoever has it may not wish to give it back to me. Whatever the outcome of my search, where I find my ring may not be a pleasant place for a lady to be.' He gave a sigh. 'It is safer for you to wait here for my return.'

Unable to believe what she was hearing, Amy replied with a slight scold in her voice.

'You obviously consider yourself free

to put yourself in danger, so whatever you feel you must do is important. Important enough even to postpone our wedding night — a most unfortunate beginning to our marriage!'

Charles sounded contrite as he explained, 'I beg your forgiveness, Amy. It is not as though I wanted this to happen tonight, of all nights. I would wish that when we make love, it will not be a hurried affair, especially as I respect you too much to treat you . . . '

Like what? Amy wondered and was only glad he did not say what she had guessed.

'You wish to treat me gently, then? Like a virgin bride?' she said calmly.

Smiling, he took her into his arms. 'Indeed.'

Comforted to feel he was being sincere, she leaned into him.

'Thank you for understanding, Amy.'

Their embrace was blissful but did not last long. His kiss was hungry, but not lingering.

'Our honeymoon is only delayed. But

I must go now and prepare to travel.'

Amy kept her arms around him, however, knowing that she must insist upon accompanying him. Waiting for him to return, perhaps for weeks, would be agony. And what would everyone think of her being left on her wedding night? It was like being jilted!

'Charles, I beg you, please allow me to decide my own destiny. I wish to stay with you, not to be left behind. I do not expect the comforts a lady might expect. Only being with you, and seeing France, will be my reward.'

He firmly pushed her away, saying, 'I will not allow you to be put in any danger or even made to suffer inconveniences.'

Amy looked up at his concerned expression and loved the genuineness she saw there.

'I thank you for your concern about my welfare and truly I do understand know how important it is for you to protect me, the prospective mother of your heir.'

'Amy, I do not think of you like that! I have come to respect you, admire you . . .'

Love me?

She was disappointed he could not seem to say those two simple words. Then her common sense kicked in. Was she expecting too much? Had not she achieved a great deal in his genuine concern for her, his kindness, his fortune, status and title? If he did not feel he loved her now, perhaps in time he would. When he made love to her was surely his prerogative? She would have to be patient.

'Charles, we are both aware of why we married. The intimate part of our nuptials will have to be delayed. But there it is. I accept that. My insistence on travelling with you is that I have all my life looked after my mother and sister, and now I feel you need me to look after you — '

He turned away from her her abruptly and stomped around the room saying, 'I appreciate your concern for me, but as a Calvary Officer, I am more than used to looking after myself.'

'You did not at Waterloo!'

'No, I grant you, but accidents will happen. A soldier has to be prepared for that. However, you are under no obligation to put yourself in danger. I know not what the situation may be over there.'

'I know that. But I selfishly desire the opportunity to travel.'

'Your wish to travel will be satisfied when I return, I promise.'

Amy tried another tactic. 'Then you must accept that if you go without me, I will follow you.'

He stared at her, inhaled deeply and grunted.

Coming up to her and placing his large hands on her slight shoulders he boomed, 'All right, all right! I cannot stop you if you are so determined. But are you quite sure you wish to come with me tonight, not knowing where you might land up, not knowing the unstable political state of France in the northern region?'

For the second time that day, Amy knew she was committing herself to God knew what.

'I am,' she said firmly. 'Yes, I am.'

She said so because she felt she had come to love him. She *did* want to be with him as much as she wanted to travel. She did not wish to stay behind, alone in this house she did not know, waiting for news of him and wondering what he was doing, or even if he lived. Nevertheless she was apprehensive of what lay ahead.

He bowed his head, saying, 'I will not be the kind of husband who overrules your wishes and dictates how you should live your life. It was not part of our bargain that if you married me I should prevent you from doing as you please, Amy. I can only warn you of the possible hazards of travel . . . '

She looked up into his eyes and they spoke to her of his honesty.

'I am prepared to take those risks. I married you because I . . . because I want to be with you.'

'For better or worse?'

'Exactly that!'

He looked at her with softness in his eyes and, taking her in his arms he pressed her head against his chest saying, 'If you insist on coming with me, I can only admire your loyalty to me, Amy, and I promise you that I will try to be worthy of it, and look after you as best as I am able.'

His kiss was like sealing another bargain.

'Now we must quickly turn our minds to the practicalities of our immediate departure . . . on our bridal tour, eh?'

★   ★   ★

A holiday honeymoon she thought was not unusual, a thrilling adventure she looked forward to, although Charles had warned her it would be no picnic. She thought maybe he saw it as his duty to warn her of any dangers, and to expect travel to be a little uncomfortable at times. It could be dangerous too with highwaymen about, and wheels coming loose and rolling off carriages. Or the carriage landing up in a ditch when two vehicles were not sufficiently careful passing one another on the slippery, muddy roads.

Yet Charles seemed not to want her to come with him. He would have to accept that he hadn't married a simpering doll. She was a modern woman with a mind of her own, and wanted him to know that from the start of their life together.

It also made Amy think that, if things became difficult for her on the journey, she would have no one to blame but herself!

With so many preparations to do quickly before they set off for the coast that night, it did not occur to Amy to ask Charles why his signet ring was so important to him, why he seemed to be risking life and limb, as he had done fighting at Waterloo. Especially after he'd been badly injured.

A ring was replaceable, surely? Although, if it was an family heirloom, perhaps not. It still did not make sense to her that a nobleman — who could always buy another — would value it so highly. She would have to ask him about this ring.

Her young maid, Molly, was obstinate when she was told of her mistress's plans to go abroad that very night and leave her behind.

'I'm coming to look after you,' Molly said, stamping her foot. 'Ladies can't look after themselves — and don't you say otherwise.'

Amy ignored her maid's rudeness, which would have cost Molly her job with most high-bred ladies. Amy however was amused, and touched, that Molly seemed to care about her and wanted to look after her mistress even in completely strange surroundings. Being young, Molly might also have a yearning for adventure.

Understanding the girl's point that

most ladies were separated from many of the daily hardships endured by their staff who supported them, and Molly's concern for what she might face, Amy was grateful. Although it was her duty to warn Molly in turn that her holiday might be hazardous.

'I'm not saying I don't want you to come, Molly. No, it is that you might be in danger — now what will your mama and your aunt say about that?'

Molly's eyes were dancing as she laughed.

'So you think they might forbid me to go with you? Heavens, no! I am used to roughing it but you're not. My mam and auntie will say I'm your maid now and must do as you wish and that I ought be with you, looking after you. And I want to. It'll be exciting for me to leave London for a jaunt abroad, my lady.'

It was a shock for Amy to hear herself called 'my lady' and yet she knew she would have to get used to it. She also knew Molly would be a cheerful companion and would indeed know how to manage in some circumstances where she might feel out of her depth.

So, just as Charles had allowed her to come with him, Amy relented, and agreed to take her spirited maid abroad with her to face whatever happened to them — and be thankful for her companionship.

It was not a summer holiday she was embarking on, Amy reminded herself as she and Molly packed her travel bag. She may not get the chance to wash or change her linens often, and her well-worn woollens would be all the more welcome on a cold day as the autumn progressed, but she had the sense to keep her bag light.

Not wishing to keep Charles waiting, the women rushed to join him.

⋆ ⋆ ⋆

The carriage journey to the coast was fast and bumpy. Molly rode with the coachman, huddled in a blanket, so that the newlyweds could be alone together in the carriage.

Charles, who was now dressed in plain travelling clothes as a journeyman might wear, had no servant with him.

Amy noticed he kept looking at her as he sat opposite her in the carriage, as though he was unsure that he should be allowing her to come. Almost as though he couldn't quite believe what kind of person he'd married.

Would he ever understand her? Or she, him?

'Where are we going?' Amy said, breaking into his reverie.

'All I know for certain at present is that we will be making for Lille, which is just inside the French border. I have my scout meeting me there who tells me an informer knows the whereabouts of the ring I seek to get back.'

His hand flicked back the carriage window curtain so that he could see the twilight darkening outside as it sped by.

'Try and rest, Amy.' He leaned forward and placed his hands over on her gloved hands. 'I should like to call you Amy, and you may like to call me Charlie, as my relatives and friends do.'

It felt as if they were entering into the first intimacies of marriage. Amy smiled and nodded her approval. They were shifting to a new understanding of each other.

'Of course,' she said. 'Amy and Charlie sound far less formal — and I like the new names we have to seal our love.'

He blinked and shifted his body.

'Amy, I will always treat you with the respect you deserve, but can you say that you love me? I, a man who has snatched you away from the safety of your childhood home and married you in haste for his own purposes — and then proposes to cast you into the unknown?'

'That sounds rather brutally honest, Charlie, and I suppose it is. However, it has been my own choice, remember. I had have my own reasons to wish to take this bridal tour. I have always longed to see more of the world, warts and all.'

'So be it.'

He leaned back on his cushioned carriage seat. But he gave her a wonderful smile that lit up his face as if to thank her.

She wished he would say that he loved her, although maybe he was being honest, because he did not.

He told her, 'I will do my utmost to make you comfortable — you have my word on it — but there are bound to be some ups and downs.'

Not expecting any more endearments towards her she replied, 'Surely that is marriage, Charlie, even if a bride and groom do not recognise it at first. Material comforts are not as essential as true affection that can weather all storms. Will my sister Harriet and your friend Horatio be any happier on their honeymoon, surrounded by comforts they have?'

He smiled. 'Unless you wish it was Horatio's bed you might be sleeping in?'

'Charlie!'

'My apologies. Past loves are past loves — I said it myself, after all. Shall we agree on that?'

'Yes, indeed we shall.'

Again she longed for him to say he loved her, but he did no more than smile at her. He was like a mountain she had to climb — it would take time!

One comfort she did have in her heart was that she felt her previous love affair with Horatio was now completely over. Lord Charles Chard now satisfied her entirely. He was turning out to be the kind of husband she could admire and trust. She judged him to be a true gentleman, far better than she could ever have imagined she could marry. At least . . . she hoped that was so.

'Take some rest,' he ordered as he closed his eyes and stretched out his long legs.

Amy closed her eyes and tried to relax her body and still the tumultuous thoughts in her mind.

So much had happened to her

recently — some happenings she had brought on herself, but others had been suddenly added. She was both excited and bewildered, yet she felt blessed because she was certain Charlie was genuinely a good man. Her choice to stay with him through thick and thin was her own decision.

She did sleep a little eventually and was awakened as the horses were being halted.

Looking out of the carriage window she could see at first nothing but the darkness of night. The salty air and the cries of seagulls told her they had reached the coast.

Lord Charles had leaped out of the carriage, leaving the coachman to assist Amy and Molly down the carriage steps. The autumn sharpness in the air hit her as she dismounted and the coastal wind howled and tugged at her travel cloak, which was a well-worn hand-me-down from her mother and did little to keep her warm.

Seagulls flying around them and the

roar of the breakers crashing against the little harbour seawall assailed her senses — as did the smell of rotten fish. After a while her eyes became accustomed to the moonlit darkness and she could make out an inn where the horses were being taken by a stable lad, and she could see a fleet of fishing boats bobbing about on the water.

This was no major port, merely a small fisherman's village they had arrived at.

Charlie had begun bargaining with a fisherman to obtain a Channel crossing. She observed from all the hand gestures and raised voices that the captain of the boat was not keen to make the crossing that night and was taking more than a little persuasion. Could not his lordship wait until dawn? the captain wanted to know.

Amy had never seen the sea before and began to feel a little . . . well, afraid. The vastness of it as the moon lit up its angry swell gave some indication that the crossing would be no pleasant sailing expedition — not like a punt on the calm waters of a lake, the extent of her experience.

She swallowed hard. Was it too late to change her mind? Possibly her husband would be pleased if she did, yet the urge to stay with him — perish with him, if that was to be her fate — remained strong with her.

Perhaps it was just as well that there was no time to agonise over her decision as she observed a couple of seamen appearing to assist the skipper. A fishing boat was hastily being prepared to set sail. Presumably Charlie had, in his haste to get abroad, offered the seamen a very generous fee.

★ ★ ★

Around midnight their sea crossing was finally arranged in the sturdy fishing vessel, smelling unpleasantly of decaying fish, but the skipper and his mate seemed anxious to please their honoured passengers and offered them the use of their tiny cabin on the vessel.

Charlie remarked that the only berth would make Amy a bed, and when Molly her maid went to collect their travel bags, he remarked, 'I fear your young maid has a flighty nature; she has already made friends with the captain's mate.'

Amy smiled. 'Yes, I had noticed her chatting with him, but I assure you I am satisfied with her. I believe she has a bold spirit and a good heart.'

'Very well, Amy — we can perhaps find you a better lady's maid when we get to the Kingdom of the Netherlands, our destination. There I will meet the man who has news about my ring.'

Having settled their sailing arrangements, the last thing that Amy expected when her maid appeared carrying the travel bags was to see her dog being led up to the boat too.

'Skippy!' she breathed, amazed to see the animal. She was glad to have something from home to take with her, yet also distraught that she had forgotten the poor animal and had left no instruction about how the dog was to be looked after while she was abroad. No one had told her whether he had been left at Chard's home with the servants or sent back to her mother's house.

'We cannot take that animal!' Lord Chard shouted suddenly.

Amy bristled. 'We cannot leave Skippy behind.'

It was a clash of wills. Amy loved Charlie, but she loved her dog too. Who would look after the poor animal if she did not? He would be a stray by the seaside, rejected, starving, far away from his home. Amy would not let Skippy suffer that.

Molly seemed unaware of the conflict over the dog, determined to bring the animal on board anyway, and the dog was wagging its tail as if he fully expected to join them on the journey.

'I did not know that my dog had been sent with my luggage, I promise you, Charles. But I will not leave him here abandoned — it would be cruel,' she informed her husband.

He had stormed over towards her and stood glaring down as though determined to win this battle, but Amy knew his kind heart would not allow the dog to be harmed.

So she looked up into his fierce eyes and said, 'When you married me, you took my goods and chattels — and Skippy is one of them.'

'I'll look after him,' piped up Molly, giving the dog an affectionate stroke.

'Get aboard then,' Chard said angrily, grabbing Amy's hand in a familiar way and pulling her towards the boat, where he jumped down into the vessel and then lifted her off the harbour wall and placed her down beside him. Then he grabbed the dog, who seemed happy to be in his arms, and placed the animal by Amy's feet.

With the luggage and passengers on board, the fishermen shouted and the craft rocked violently as it was pushed away from the harbour berth.

For better or worse they were on

their way to . . . well, Amy was unsure what lay ahead!

As she lay on her narrow and uncomfortable berth, feeling queasy as the sea rocked her, she wondered whether her husband was very angry with her for insisting on taking the dog.

It was the first time she had crossed him and he obviously did not like it. He had not come to keep her company in the little cabin during the voyage, and where the animal had been taken to lie down to rest, she had no idea. Nor, for that matter, did she know where Molly was. Her young maid had a mind of her own.

If Molly had made friends with one of the crew as Charles had told her she had, did it matter if Molly was a friendly soul? A conventional, properly trained servant would not behave like that, but only do what was considered correct for a lady's maid. Yet Molly promised to be different — an independent character — and Amy could only hope she would also be a loyal one.

6

When morning came Amy was thankful to have slept, despite her churning stomach, during the choppy sea journey. But she was burdened with the worry about her husband after their first disagreement — and concern for a maid who, it would appear, had vanished!

Going up on deck, she was ignored by the crew who were occupied mooring the boat. Charlie was nowhere to be seen, and there was no sign of Molly or her dog either. Gingerly, and without help, Amy managed to climb up and out of the boat onto the quay. It was not an elegant manoeuvre for a lady, but who in this foreign land was paying any attention to her, or even knew who she was?

A gusty wind blew her cloak around her body, making her shiver. However, the sights and sounds she saw absorbed her.

In some ways the scene did not look so very different from the English fisherman's village they had left last night — and yet it was. The houses looked different, some with larger windows and shutters. The people on the quay were dressed in their native costume — they wore distinctive hats and clomped on the cobbled ground in wooden clogs — and she could not understand what they were saying.

Amy blinked as the sun came out and she shaded her eyes as she gazed around. This was a working community, nothing grand to be seen.

It certainly wasn't going to be the luxurious life of a noblewoman she had envisaged a few days ago. There was no maid to bring her an early morning cup of tea or coffee. No jug of hot water to wash with, or fresh clothes for her to wear. In the hustle and bustle of their working lives, the people of the Kingdom of the Netherlands paid hardly any attention to the plainly dressed English tourists who had arrived by boat that morning.

Jolted, Amy felt abandoned, and reminded herself that she had no one to blame but herself for her present unhappy circumstances, so she had best simply accept whatever else fate had in store for her.

Lord Chard did not delay. After paying the skipper of the fishing boat, he assembled his little band on the fishing village wharf, huddled together, and began to look around for transport. This he found quite quickly, though it was merely a roughly made farm cart. Amy suspected it was only due to the high price he was prepared to pay for it that they even had that.

'This farmer came into this harbour to sell his farm produce early this morning. Now he has sold it, he is returning to his farm, but has agreed to make a detour to give us a lift to Lille,' explained Charlie, who seemed in no mood to discuss anything with his wife, simply telling her what she must do.

Amy, Molly and the dog were lifted into the grimy, smelly farm cart, alongside boxes of fish which the driver was taking back to his village in exchange for the farm produce he'd brought to the quay earlier that morning.

Sitting on a box in the cart, while Charlie sat with the driver, Amy felt chilly, but looked with absorbed interest at the low-lying countryside they were soon travelling through. There was something about the morning light on the countryside that was special to the region — huge skies with billowing white, grey, and mauve clouds. They passed dykes and waterways, huge watermills, their blades whirring as they turned.

She had been told they were on their way to the French border and the town of Lille. She longed to ask Charles why they were making for Lille, but thinking herself still in his bad books for her insisting on bringing Skippy, she refrained. She would no doubt learn soon enough.

★   ★   ★

When they arrived at the border, the French border guards were more interested in their breakfast than in looking at the humble carts of travellers passing by. In fact, it soon became clear to Amy that they were not the only people making their way along the highway towards the city of Lille. Their solitary cart was now joined by others. Soon they were part of a stream of people moving towards the city whose buildings could be seen in the far distance, with substantial city walls, castle turrets, domes and steeply sloping house roofs.

'It must be market day,' Amy said, now feeling more relaxed and enjoying being surrounded by a crowd of foreign voices, plodding along the road, some with laden hand carts and some herding animals with their squeals, grunts and squawks. 'I feel like a countrywoman off to sell the pies I made early this morning!'

'Just as well that you do,' Charlie commented, overhearing her remark and glancing back at her over his shoulder. 'The French have been trundling cartloads of their nobles to the guillotine so we wouldn't want any of this crowd to know we are titled!'

That sombre thought made Amy gasp. Perhaps it was just as well she was wearing her mother's old cloak, her hair undressed and shoes that had seen better days.

She understood now why Charlie had attired himself in countryman's clothes. They could mingle with the crowd without attracting notice.

Before they entered the city, Charlie directed them towards a wayside inn where they sat outside and were served fresh bread with cider. It was not the kind of breakfast Amy was used to, but she accepted that from now on she would have to be reconciled with whatever was offered, however strange to her, and not complain.

Suddenly a commotion caused her to look towards the road where a boy was bawling his head off. No one seemed to notice his distress, except for Charlie who went over to the lad and, crouching down, asked him what was the matter.

Amy went over to see if the boy had been injured. The boy sobbed that his flock of geese had been dispersed by a careless rider, and that he would have to return home with no money.

Amy said to Charlie, 'Get him to tell us where his geese are before they get lost in the country side — my dog, Skippy, will be able to round them up for him.'

Charlie put his arm around the boy's shoulders and tried to explain — which was not easy as the local patois was not the French spoken by the educated upper classes and which both she and Charlie had learned at their schools in England. However, as soon as Skippy was brought, the boy began to understand what the sheepdog was able to do.

'Find the geese,' said Amy, pointing to where she could see them grazing at a distance.

Charlie began to walk towards them and called the dog, who cocked his head with a puzzled expression, not at first understanding the need for him to round up the straying animals.

There was a great deal of interest and laughter as market folk sitting at the outdoor tables were treated to the spectacle of the English trying to teach their dog to collect the scattered geese. Although the operation was raucous and at times it seemed hopeless that Skippy would understand what he was supposed to do, eventually he did, and proceeded to skilfully round up the geese to everyone's amusement.

After the grateful boy had his little band of geese reassembled, Charlie said to Amy quietly, 'I will say no more against that dog, Amy. Skippy has earned his keep. Now we must get into the town as soon as we can. I must find my scout before he thinks I am not coming.'

Amy rejoiced that her first disagreement with her husband was over. She felt delighted when Charlie had the grace to admit that he was not right to want to abandon the dog, and the animal had come in useful after all. Also, she felt that she, as his wife, could insist on having her way — at times, at least. It made her feel closer to him as she realised his vulnerability was well as her own. They both would make mistakes at times.

★ ★ ★

Entering the medieval town, Lille's Grand Palace did not need to be pointed out as the bells were sounding, summoning people there. They joined the throng of local people hurrying to find a space to set up a stall to sell their wares.

Amy soon realised it was a huge market. The square was like a giant shop full of bric a brac with pieces of furniture, pottery, cloth and shoes, as well as farm-made butter, cheeses and a variety of fish.

Dismounting from the cart they'd been travelling in, Amy found her hand taken by Charles so that in her open-mouthed wonderment at the vibrant scene she would not be pushed and shoved and lost in the noisy crowd. She gave her other hand to Molly, who was holding onto the dog's lead and was not above giving anyone a shove if needed!

Charlie explained, 'This is an ancient market. People have been coming here for centuries to sell their farm produce, things they make, and their unwanted wares, while others come simply to find a bargain. This is where my father's signet ring was sold after the Battle of Waterloo — or so I have been told by Tom Brown. I wish to trace the trader who sold it and so I hope to discover who bought it.'

There was hardly room for them to stand in front of the palace, but it was where Lord Chard decided to stop, his eyes roving over the crowds looking to find Tom. Not seeing the man he was looking for, Charlie left Amy and Molly on the steps of the Grand Palace with strict instructions that they were to stay there until he returned. Soon her husband had disappeared among the crowd, intent on searching the market for his scout.

Left to feast her eyes on the market, Amy enjoyed the spectacle. Never before had she experienced hearing the calls and shouting of so many people in one place. It was real life as she had never imagined it after her genteel upbringing, and far more exciting than the town market she had known at home. Here she was not a titled lady, kept apart from the hoi polloi — she felt herself part of humanity.

After sitting on the palace steps for some time, Amy began to yearn to stroll through the market stalls to see what was for sale. As time went by her curiosity grew stronger. 'I wish we could go and look around,' she cried in frustration.

'His lordship does seem to be taking an age,' Molly agreed, leaping to her feet. 'Hold the dog, ma'am, and I'll go and look for him.'

Without waiting for permission, Molly thrust the dog lead into Amy's hand and was off into the crowd in a twinkling. Amy felt suddenly alone and somewhat scared. She stroked Skippy, glad of the dog's company.

A short time later Lord Chard — who was taller than most of the folk here — could be seen striding back towards her, with Molly chattering to him.

'Damned if I can think what has happened to Tom,' Charlie muttered, clearly put out. 'I shall have to stay here and wait for him.'

Molly chirped up, 'Lord Charles says we may go and look at the market, my lady.'

'Do not call us Lord and Lady,' Chard told the maid severely. 'Unless you want us carted off to prison — or worse! Please remember some French people have a great dislike for the aristocracy!'

'Yes, sir,' said Molly brightly, not in the least bothered to be reprimanded.

'Now, give me Skippy and I shall carry him,' Charlie said. 'He won't want his paws stepped on in the crush of the market.'

Thrilled to be given the chance to look around, Amy eagerly entered the busy market with Molly and mingled among the crowd. Amy's attention was soon caught by the pedlars' wares. There was so much to see — not only country goods, but here and there some beautiful furniture and furnishings.

Surprised at first to see truly valuable things for sale among the pot and pans, Amy suddenly realised that the French Revolution had seen the ransacking of many rich town houses and chateaux as their aristocratic owners were carted off to the guillotine! Local people had helped themselves to whatever they could and what they did not want for themselves was being sold at a flea market such as this.

It was sad to see some objects, made by skilled French craftsmen, spoiled — a fine table top badly scratched, or silk dresses ripped and soiled. A picture — possibly some mother's treasured portrait of her child — had been yanked out of its frame. Amy was glad the revolutionists had not taken over in England and shuddered at the thought of the treasures in Plate Hall, the Gibbon family home, being raided.

Suddenly Amy heard the sharp question, 'Is this yours?'

She turned to look at Molly who held her purse. Her mischievous eyes were dancing as she shook the gold coins Charlie had given Amy inside it.

Immediately Amy patted the side of her skirt where normally her purse hung from a tape. It wasn't there!

'Oh Molly — my purse has gone!'

'I caught the blighter who pinched it,' Molly said triumphantly. 'And I made her give me back your money, an' all.'

Amy felt quite sick. Her enjoyment of the market ceased abruptly as she was suddenly faced with how vulnerable she was in this jostling crowd of foreigners. Of course she'd heard of pickpockets, but having lived in the countryside all her life it was not an evil she had personally encountered.

She was far away from the safety of England now and felt defenceless, yet thankful for her quick-witted little maid as she tied her purse back securely to the tape around her waist that had been cut by the pickpocket. She now knew she had to be more alert to constant danger in future.

The booming bells of the nearby church reminded her that the time had passed quickly as they were enjoying looking at the market wares, and they should return to the palace steps.

'My goodness, how the time has flown, Molly,' she said. 'We must have been wandering around the market for over an hour. We must run back quickly. His lordship will be cross that we have taken so long.'

He was. They found Lord Chard pacing the front of the palace. Nearby him stood a sinewy man who had been given the dog's lead, as Skippy sat by his feet.

As Amy approached, Charlie strode over towards her and boomed, 'Dear God, madam, where have you been?'

Amy was taken aback by the look of fury in his eyes. He had been kept waiting and he did not like it. He came up very close to her and she thought for a moment he might slap her!

Amy stuttered, 'I am sorry, Charles. I was simply so interested in seeing what was in the market that time just slipped by and — '

'You do realise that I am in a hurry to start searching for my ring?'

The sarcasm in his voice made her cross.

'Of course I do!' she snapped.

'Then, madam, perhaps you also realise that if I cannot find it you will suffer as much as I?'

No, she had not understood the meaning of that. Why should his ring mean anything to her? But as Amy had no wish to start another quarrel with him, she did not ask what he meant. It was clear he was restless and understandably angry to be held up by her carelessness with the time, and she could not blame him for that.

He went on, 'Surely you know that when you are among traders and a crowd interested in their old wares, buying and selling anything, there are likely to be rogues among them? I would have thought you would be aware of the possible danger you might be in — and that I would be worried about you?'

Colouring under his scrutiny, she made a great effort to look up into his glare.

'Indeed I do. In fact, my purse was stolen, but Molly was able to retrieve it for me. It has taught me a valuable lesson and I am determined to be more careful in future.'

'See that you are!'

Seeing her tearful eyes, Lord Chard refrained from scolding her any more.

He gave a nod of thanks to Molly, who beamed back at him.

'Come and meet Tom Brown,' he said. 'He is an Englishman who scouted for Wellington, and has traced my ring. He will be escorting us near to where he believes it is.'

Approaching Tom Brown, Amy was able to believe that although he was a young man, he was also an experienced ex-soldier. His weathered skin showed his life had been spent out in the open. His constantly moving eyes were alert, but not so obtrusive as to make her feel uncomfortable as she assessed him. Attired in baggy trousers and a none-too-clean shirt and jacket, with a hat over his long, unkempt hair, he could have been mistaken for someone's servant. A man who could hide himself among the crowd.

'Lady Chard,' Tom said, removing his hat as he bowed to greet her.

Amy remembered not to bob a curtsy that might give her status away, but she liked the courtesy he showed, and had no doubt he was, as Charlie had told her, a man with scouting skills.

Charlie told her that Tom had knowledge of where they had to go but explained, 'First we must stay here for the night in Lille, as there will be no inns where we are going.'

Amy did not fancy staying the night at the rough-looking tavern the men chose, which was surrounded by noisy local people dining at the end of the day.

However, she was glad to sit down on a wooden bench, not being treated like a mistress with her maid or Charlie as a lord with his servant, as the four of them sat down to eat together. Instead of feeling awkward, Amy appreciated the comfort of companionship. She also enjoyed her soup and a platter of freshly-made bread with mussels, a local and popular fish dish.

She made sure the dog was fed too as Charles was engaged in talking to Tom about their plans for their next move.

Amy guessed there would be uncomfortable times ahead. Well, she had wanted an adventurous holiday with her honeymoon, had she not?

7

Charlie, who was sitting next to Amy, suddenly turned and put his arm around her, talking to her confidentially as if he didn't want anyone nearby to hear what he was saying. Such physical familiarity, even between husband and wife, would not be acceptable in public under the strict rules of English Society, but they were far from being censured. Amy liked it, as it showed her that Charlie had forgiven her for keeping him waiting — and that he had been genuinely worried about her earlier that afternoon.

He began to explain in a hushed voice, 'Tom tells me my ring is in the possession of an unscrupulous man who is using it on documents promising my father will pay the money. My father will soon be without funds unless I claim it back.'

Ah — that was the nub of it, then.

Although cheques were now being used by banks, a nobleman's signet ring seal could, under some circumstances, still be used like a signature on a debtor's promise-to-pay paper document.

Now Amy understood the urgency of finding the earl's ring, and the worry Charlie had of it being used to blacken his father's name and steal his wealth — and Charlie, being his father's heir, would lose his inheritance as the earl's bank was honouring the bills by paying them.

It had to be stopped!

'I must get the ring back from this fraudster as quickly as possible.' It made sense to Amy, as Charlie went on to explain, 'You will understand, I am sure, that after the turmoil of the Revolution, momentous changes took place in French society. Napoleon, a great administrator, began to put things in order so that the country was well governed. He restored the monarchy. However . . . ' Charlie declared bluntly,

'Napoleon was also a warlike leader who took his soldiers to war until he was finally defeated and imprisoned.'

Life must, Amy reasoned, have been turbulent in the extreme for people in France after Waterloo, with many ex-soldiers and deserters roaming around trying to find food and shelter. Where the previous French land owners had been killed or disinherited, some rogues could flourish — especially in the north of France during the aftermath of Waterloo, and the defeat of Napoleon. Although an Army of Occupation was now in place to prevent further conflict, many of the French had had to adjust their lives, with some losing, and some gaining, wealth.

Amy had seen in the market place things that had belonged in chateaux and other aristocratic homes that had been wrecked and goods stolen. Amy sensed the unease around her, the lack of certainty, after the great social upheaval.

Turning her eyes to look up at the

now familiar and loved features of her husband, she asked, 'What are you planning to do?'

Charlie clearly had no plan. He was relying on his scout to direct the party.

He replied, 'We must allow Tom to guide us to the chateau where he tells me the man who has my papa's ring is living.'

'But I thought the local aristocracy and gentry had been imprisoned?'

'Many were. Regretfully the marquis and his family, who lived in the chateau we are going to, were slaughtered by the mob during the Revolution. But the marquis's secretary is still living there. Monsieur Lenoir is intelligent, well-educated, and able to convince people that he will stand surety by using the ring to buy what he wishes with it. He has also assembled a band of brigands around him. Ruffians, army deserters, I've been told, and all ruthless men. A nest of rats, so Tom tells me they are, who have caused no end of misery to people living nearby.'

Amy blinked. She could imagine the state of the place, with many ruffians living in the once elegant rooms. How easily the estate would become run-down when the owners had been forced to leave their home. The farm land would be neglected and former servants too would be out of work — a disaster for many local people.

Charlie, understanding Amy could now appreciate how the leader of the brigands was stealing goods to live on and sending the bills to Earl Collingwood, said no more about it.

Taking a deep breath, Amy looked with sympathy at Charlie. What a fix he was in!

He was so near reaching his goal and yet, realising the almost impossible task of retrieving the ring, he was clearly distraught. Yet he could not abandon his quest. He had to somehow regain possession of his father's signet ring.

She placed her hand over his and said, 'I am sorry for it, but you will have trouble getting your papa's ring back.'

She deliberately chose not to say she thought him unable — she knew the challenge of his quest was burning inside him.

Charlie said, 'Now you know the dangerous situation, you must remain here in Lille, Amy. Or I can arrange for you and your maid to be taken to Calais tomorrow where you can get the ferry back to England — '

'No! I will stay with you.' She looked up at him stubbornly. Afraid to be left alone when he would go off to search for the ring, and also feeling he was somehow vulnerable — his former sheltered life had not prepared him for making decisions and hardships. He was relying on Tom to direct him. But sooner or later he would be faced with having to cope on his own.

He had great strength of character, of that she felt sure, but Amy felt she wanted to be available in case she could be of any help to him. Her previous life had not been as easy as his had been; therefore, she saw her duty as a wife who supported him and did not run away when circumstances became difficult. Not that she thought he would do anything rash, but they were in difficult territory at present.

His voice rose. 'My dear girl, you have no idea how harsh camping can be! Besides, Tom and I are not sure how long it will take us to get the ring. We may find it difficult to know who to trust in the neighbourhood, or even where to find something to eat. All kinds of difficulties may occur — and the weather will be getting colder. Amy, you don't wish to suffer from these hardships, do you?'

His slight smile annoyed her.

Certainly, she did not! However, she was sure that whatever his destiny, it would be hers too.

She also understood now the necessity for her husband to hide his identity and of being a rich aristocrat or he might find himself at the mercy of a mob and robbed. He had to play the part of a gentleman only interested in visiting France for some reason other than what he intended to do. And she would have to play her part.

Tom, who had been chatting to Molly, showing their warm liking for one another, now switched his attention to the argument between Charlie and his wife, so he overheard Amy insisting she should stay with them.

'Can you ride?' Tom butted in to ask Amy.

'Yes,' she replied. 'I had a pony as a child. My sister and I went riding daily until my father died and our reduced finances meant we had to empty the stables.'

Tom then asked her, 'Are you able to take your maid up with you?'

Amy said she thought she would, if the pace was steady.

'Then we'll stay here for the night, and continue our journey in the morning on horseback as we need the daylight to travel through the woods — we want to avoid being seen on the roads.'

★　★　★

They were enjoying some excellent French wine after their meal, and the party relaxed. But not for long, as Amy caught sight of a pathetic-looking woman with two young children outside the tavern begging for food. She nudged Charlie who was talking to Tom and drew his attention to the poor family. But it was Tom who rose and called to the landlord, asking him to provide the unfortunates with food and shelter.

Returning to the table he explained, 'It makes me angry to see families like that who have been thrown out of their homes.'

'What will happen to them?' Amy asked.

'There's a convent in Lille where they will be cared for by the good nuns. But they should not have lost their home. I expect it was the local brigands who caused the family harm. Since I have been in this region I have heard of many local peasants who had their livelihood destroyed, because these brigands steal from them. They demand a poor farmer's cattle, pigs and chickens for their food, and fodder for their horses, not paying for what they take. Consequently some of the peasants are starving.'

Amy and Charlie exchanged looks of dismay on hearing this, as Tom went on to tell them about the acts of cruelty, even murder, inflicted by these brigands. The very same brigands they had to get the signet ring from! It made Amy shiver. And when he continued to describe how some young women had been kidnapped and forced to work for the brigands, Charlie protested, putting up his hand to silence him. 'Enough, Tom!'

'Can the authorities not prevent it?' cried Amy, distressed to hear of the criminals' activities.

'They would if they could,' Charlie replied. 'But as you are aware, the French have yet to re-establish order in all of this region. Robbers and army deserters have banded together under a ruthless, yet clever leader.'

'Who is the leader of these brigands?' enquired Amy.

Tom replied brusquely, 'The same villain who has the signet ring your husband is looking for, ma'am. Monsieur Lenoir, they call him.'

A horrified silence descended on them. Understanding how cruel these men could be, Amy shivered to think of the danger they would be in if any of the brigands should catch them!

Charlie took hold of Amy's chin gently and made her look directly into his eyes.

'Now you know what we are up against. Would you not prefer to go back to England tomorrow?'

She gulped.

'Charlie, I have told you many times, no! Your father expects you to reclaim his ring and I know you will do your best to get it. As your wife, travelling with you, the brigands should not bother us, especially as we do not appear to be rich and worth robbing. They will ignore us.'

Charlie shook his head, before he released her chin. 'I only hope you are right!'

Amy could tell her husband was not pleased with her decision.

She thought he did not want the worry of her tagging along — not that he loved her or would miss her company as she would miss him. But what if she was being stupidly obstinate, risking the success of his mission by insisting that she went with him? Possibly he was afraid she might make a fuss if he was to insist she stayed behind. The last thing he would want was for everyone at the tavern to hear them arguing when they were supposed to be lying low.

Getting her own way might result in a disaster. How would she feel if he was right, and he was doing the sensible thing in telling her she should return to England in the morning?

Even worse, what if she, or any of them, were captured by these villains? She would be responsible for their capture.

Molly suddenly pushed back her chair and stood up. 'Come along, ma'am. It's time for ladies to retire.'

What awaited her was not the kind of accommodation Amy was used to. Their tavern attic room was far from clean, as was the bed. However, Amy felt so tired that she slept soundly in spite of it, with her loyal maid by her side.

8

Next morning, Amy had no time to reconsider her decision. Charlie ignored her, as if cross with her — which wounded her feelings because she still believed she was going to help him.

After finishing their breakfast, the mounted party set off on ponies which Tom had hired for them. He led the way out of the city and headed towards a forest. Amy began to feel apprehensive as they left the security of the city behind.

The beautiful countryside delighted her, however. The rich greens of the trees just showing signs of the autumn colouring shone in the sunlight. Birds and forest creatures gave life to the ever-changing scene as they followed Tom deep into the forest.

The ride took them all day with only brief stops for refreshments which they carried in their saddlebags. As twilight engulfed them it made the path through the woodland difficult to see but Tom seemed to know exactly where they were heading. Charlie kept Skippy under control so that he did not dart off chasing rabbits.

The girls were almost dropping off their pony in fatigue after such a long ride that they were not used to, when finally they arrived at what appeared to be a woodman's cottage.

'This is no comfortable inn to spend the night,' remarked Tom, 'but it has been uninhabited since the Revolution, and it is near the chateau where we must go to search for the ring.'

No cottage could have looked more deprived than the one they entered. Whoever had lived there before it was abandoned must have been the poorest of the poor. The whole cottage was little more than a shed, with the roughest of furniture and the pathetic remains of textiles and cooking equipment.

Amy could not help but contrast the

poverty of the dwelling with the grand house nearby, where luxury and extravagance had been the norm.

Tom had read her thoughts.

'The aristocrat who owned this estate was executed, and his family fled the chateau years ago. The house and estate has suffered from neglect as the workers left too, but now the brigands have taken over.

'Their leader, Monsieur Lenoir, used to be the marquis' secretary — and he is a tyrant. The villagers who remained here fear him and his band of men. They feel helpless to remove him and suffer more than they ever did when the aristocrat owned the estate.

'The tales I've heard of his brigands' crimes . . . ' He looked at the women's woeful faces and hesitated to relate all he heard had happened, but went on, 'Lenoir has possession of Lord Chard's ring which came up for sale at the Lille market and he has been using it to buy all he can get his hands on, making Earl Collingwood pay for his debts.'

Reminded of the urgency of their quest to obtain the ring, and dispirited at finding themselves unable to think of a plan to actually retrieve it, the group — who were tired and already despondent about their shelter — looked at each other aghast. There was no meal for them, or beds with clean sheets. The situation was dire — and Amy, for one, had no idea what could be done about getting the signet ring back.

Tom went on to say, 'I do not think Lord Chard should approach Monsieur Lenoir openly and demand his ring back, as he would be attacked or even killed by one of his ruffians for sure. I think we must enter the chateau and steal the ring.'

'Will not Monsieur Lenoir be wearing it?'

'That I know not . . . but I do not believe even Lenoir would dare wear it during the day. It is too conspicuous. And he would, I feel sure, take it off at night and put it somewhere he would think it would be safe as it is too valuable for him to lose.'

They all nodded, murmuring agreement.

Tom went on, 'I have scouted around the building and found out the room where Lenoir sleeps. There are no guards posted anywhere in the chateau because the brigands do not expect to be disturbed. But there is a possibility some of his men might be up during the night drinking, playing cards . . . or whoring.'

Amy gulped. Tom had not mentioned in detail what these bandits did to their captives, but she shivered, thinking of what they might do to her if she were to be caught by them!

Charlie was looking distraught. They had come all this way only now to find it impossible for him to retrieve his father's ring, and his quest seemed hopeless.

Amy put her head on one side as she looked at him, sympathetic to see him looking so downcast. She wished she could comfort him. That was why she had come, after all, but at that moment she felt he was almost hostile towards her because she had not stayed behind at the tavern, where he felt she would be better off than where they were now in a tumbledown, cold, meagre cottage.

Molly was thinking along different lines.

'My lord, let me go and climb up on the roof and let myself down one of the chimneys and take a look for the key. I've done some chimney sweeping when I was a little 'un. I used to go with my brother, who was working for a sweep until he grew too big. I could easily get into Lenoir's bedchamber and look for the ring.'

Charlie looked at the maid in astonishment.

'I thank you, Molly — but I will not allow you to put yourself in such danger.'

Tom suggested they were all tired and that they should eat and then get some rest. Perhaps an idea for recovering the ring might occur to them in the morning.

Accustomed to camping, Tom soon lit a fire, while Charlie tended the ponies and brought out some provisions from the saddle bags. They ate in near silence, fed the dog, and lay down upon the hard earth, huddled together and covered only by a soldier's blanket.

Amy was too sore and exhausted to stay awake even in those deprived conditions.

★   ★   ★

A wild creature's cry woke Amy as the first light of the morning brightened the sky.

Stiffness from chilled limbs and sleeping on the hard floor quickly brought her to her senses. But it was Molly shaking her that made her sit up.

'I got it!' Molly crowed, as loud as a cockerel.

Before her very eyes, Amy saw that Molly held a golden ring with a gleaming red jewel in her blackened fingers. The ring looked magnificent

— not merely a beautiful ornament, but an emblem of power.

Amy immediately knew the danger Molly had been in — her maid had obviously been to the chateau during the night, climbed down the chimney, as she had said she could, found and snatched the ring, and then brought it back!

'Molly!' Amy almost slapped her for taking such a risk but she laughed instead. 'Oh, Molly, you naughty girl, you disobeyed my husband!'

Her sooty blackened face, hair and clothes told Amy that Molly had done exactly what she had suggested she could do.

During the night, the little maid had climbed up onto the roof of the chateau, deduced which was the chimney that led down to the bedroom Lenoir used, and climbed down it like a chimney sweep. She had then searched his bedroom until she discovered where he had secreted the ring. She had seized it, then climbed the chimney steps once more and made her way down from the roof — all without being caught or even falling!

Overwhelmed that her maid had been so determined, so brave, Amy felt tears come to her eyes. Bereft of anything she could say to thank her sincerely, and despite the soot all over her, she hugged the girl.

Then reality struck her.

'We must leave with all speed, Molly, before Lenoir wakes and realises the ring is missing and sends his men to search for us. Rouse the men quickly to saddle the horses. We must collect our things and go immediately. We shall have to wait to wash the soot off later, when we are far away from the chateau. And we must prevent Skippy from barking!'

Soldiers both men had been, not unused to being woken suddenly in an emergency, and they immediately sprang into action.

'My ring!' Chard was clearly overwhelmed to have it placed in his hand.

He did not put it on his finger, but instead concealed it in the inside watch pocket of his waistcoat.

Tom, impressed by the daring young maid's midnight theft from the chateau, smiled as he nodded his head approvingly.

Then he shouted, 'We must get away from here at once! Lenoir will be looking for us.'

He darted around, collecting their camping things and removing any evidence of them being in the cottage overnight.

While Tom was busy, Charlie quickly helped prepare the ponies for their departure — after he had caught hold of Molly's small, sooty hand and kissed it, saying, 'You have my undying gratitude.'

'Get away, my Lord!' retorted Molly, smiling proudly. 'You'd have done the same if you could only have got up and down them chimneys, but you're too big to squeeze down them narrow corridors.'

Watching Charlie thanking her maid, Amy saw him brush away a tear from his eye. The signet ring was not mere jewellery to him. It was, as with most people who owned any jewellery, valued for sentimental reasons and more. That ring belonged to his father and he wanted to return it to him. It was lent to him to keep him safe in battle — and it had. Then it had been stolen and used like a bank draft and Charles was required to stop the fraud. And thanks to her cheeky, plucky little maid he now had it back.

She saw how he had changed, from presenting himself as an aloof aristocrat — no doubt in the way he had been taught to do since boyhood — into a man who could show his innermost feelings.

Amy shook herself. She had no time to stand and wonder, she knew they were far from safe now they had the precious ring, and she must concentrate on what needed to be done to assist their flight from this place. They had to convey the signet ring back to England. The brigand king Lenoir's evil men would soon be looking for the person or persons who took it. And woe betide them if they were caught!

Tom allowed them no time to even have any drink or breakfast, insisting they fly immediately. After consulting Charlie briefly as to his plan for their route, he brought forward the horses ready for them all to mount.

'We must make for the coast and catch the Calais mail packet,' Lord Chard said to the women gruffly as the emotion of the night's events altered his normal speaking voice.

Amy pretended not to notice his emotion, and gathered her things together for a quick departure, although she longed to tell him how she rejoiced in the success of their quest.

There was no time to question Molly about her extraordinary feat in obtaining the ring as their fast departure from France was urgent.

With villains on their tail, Amy was

frightened but determined not to show it, as she quickly mounted her pony with her travel bag rolled up on the back of her saddle.

With speed their aim, it was necessary for Molly to ride with Lord Chard.

Charlie must have been even more amazed and grateful to Molly than he appeared to be as, without hesitation, he hauled the soot-covered maid up on his horse behind him and set off following Tom through the woodland, calling the dog to follow them.

'It will take us two days to reach Calais. It's the nearest port for us to make for,' Tom explained to Amy. 'The brigands will be searching for us, but as they do not know who we are, or where we are heading, we have a good chance to get there unhindered, if we use the narrow animal tracks. As I know the direction we should make for, I shall lead. Lord Chard and I will, if necessary, hack down any branches so as to make space for you to follow. Fret not, ladies, for Lord Chard is armed with a pistol and is a first class marksman.'

Amy was startled to hear that last remark, but then she reasoned that he had been a captain in the army and should be so skilled.

Off they went, at as fast a pace as they could muster — Tom leading the way, Lord Chard with Molly following, with Skippy ordered to keep by his horse. Amy was in the rear, struggling to follow the others through the densely forested and brambled animal tracks.

Amy silently prayed it would be as Tom suggested. Having Tom to guide them gave her some confidence. Riding by herself, she prayed she would not lose the others in the vast forest.

She soon became aware not only of the click of their bridles, the snorts of their horses and the shuffle of the hooves through the leaves; the forest itself was alive with noises too. The rustle of the greenery in the wind, cries of the animals, big and tiny who lived there, the twitter of birds and even the far-off howl of a wolf.

Knowing they were in great danger now, the little party moved as softly as they could, in single file, as their ponies picked their way carefully along animals' tracks in the forest. The ponies stumbled now and again over broken branches hidden by fallen leaves on the forest floor.

Amy was suffering more than the others. The men had been used to rough living in the army, and Molly was young and used to a harder life as a servant. While Amy had not been living the life of a lady of leisure, nevertheless even her gentlewoman's life had provided her with comfort and regular meals that she was now missing. Her body ached and she became saddle-sore after many hours of riding she was unaccustomed to. She longed for a cup of tea or coffee — anything that was available to ease her discomfort.

She didn't complain, however. She had chosen — no, insisted — on coming abroad, although she had been warned about the privations. So she felt obliged to strive to ignore her hunger, her tiredness, her unwashed clothes, and the soreness she felt from walking and riding for far longer that she was used to.

Of course, she was also constantly afraid that they might be accosted at any moment by a party of vengeful brigands!

★　★　★

Eventually, after they reached a grassy clearing in the forest, Tom signalled for them to stop — but it was to rest the ponies. They all dismounted in silence, as Tom put his finger to his lips to ensure they did not make any noise.

Tom filled a billy can with water from a nearby stream, which had to be shared for them all to take a drink. Even Skippy, after lapping the stream water, sat on the grass panting and looking worn out, while Charlie held the ponies' bridles.

Tom tried to get some of the soot off Molly, but it was a hopeless task, as her hair and clothes were caked. She sorely needed to bathe in the stream, but Tom was clearly unable to risk them being held up while Molly washed — even though if they were accosted by the brigands her sooty appearance would show that she was no ordinary tourist as they hoped they appeared to be. Even Charlie, riding with Molly, had some soot rubbed into his clothes now.

When they reached an area where daylight penetrated the forest, as a fire or the collapse of a group of trees had made a clearing, Charlie looked across at Amy as if he understood she was suffering and sympathised. She felt he would have liked to have come over to say some comforting words, even though they both knew she was in this predicament out of choice. Not that he had intended to make her suffer, but she had been warned often enough by him that it could happen, and now that it had, she simply had to put up with it.

For how long neither of them knew. But if they could get to the coast and catch the ferry in the next couple of days, then her discomfort would be at an end.

Amy would have liked to ride with him, but he had Molly with him because the servant girl had never learned to direct a horse. Charlie's attitude towards Molly had changed; he now felt the brave little maid who had retrieved his ring deserved his protection. He showed he cared for Molly now just as he had come to care for Skippy.

Mounted again, Tom led them onwards, slowly now as the party was fatigued. Tom first, leading the way, then Charlie with Molly and finally Amy following them, as silently as possible as they wove their way through the forest paths.

As afternoon turned to dusk, Amy felt she might at any moment fall off her exhausted pony. Suddenly she found she had been asleep in the saddle and awoke with a cry.

Not realising, she had allowed her pony to wander along another path when the track had divided earlier. Terror gripped her when she found herself surrounded by the dank undergrowth with no sign of the others!

She almost screamed when a bramble scratched her cheek, but held back her anguished cry. If she made a noise it would attract the brigands if they were following them.

With admirable self-control and common sense, she slowed her pony to a stop and waited, perspiring in fear, until she thought the party would surely have missed her and begun searching for her.

After an anxious wait, and hearing a rustle in the leaves nearby and the crack of a twig, Amy almost called out but resisted. Someone was coming . . . but it could be friend or foe.

Beyond thankful to see Skippy nose his way through the bush, she breathed again. After the dog had found her and sat panting by her pony, she soon heard

Tom calling her name softly until she responded. Tom rode up, putting his finger to his lips to warn her not to make a sound. He took her pony's bridle quietly, leading the animal back to where Charlie and Molly were waiting anxiously.

Aware that Charlie could have been angry with her, she avoided looking at him, but somehow she knew he would not be cross with her any more. They now had a better understanding between them. She sensed that he knew she had nodded off out of sheer weariness and he appeared simply thankful that she had been found.

Had he, she wondered, become pleased with her ability to cope with the menacing situation they were in? Or had Charlie developed a genuine fondness for her?

9

Before long, although she was still struggling not to slip off her pony in her fatigued state, Amy was aware that Tom was leading them out of the forest and towards a village she could see over the open countryside in the distance.

As her weary mount plodded forward she raised her aching head and saw from the top of the hill that they had reached the flat line of the ocean on the horizon.

'The sea!' She gasped with relief, although she knew her suffering was far from over.

There was something invigorating and exciting about seeing the sea ahead of them. The salty smell, the cries of the seagulls and their acrobatic air dancing made Amy feel they were getting nearer home — and safety, and the comforts she was used to.

She had had her fill of her desire for adventure now. Her former disregard for looking her best and having the food she was used to had been transformed into a longing for those things. She yearned for the uneventfulness of her normal life — and yet, she knew even when she returned to England that her life would be utterly different. Being a married woman — and married to a viscount — was the new challenge she faced. However, she felt more sure than ever that she had married a man she loved, which was reassuring.

She had achieved her goals — to marry and to travel abroad — and so had Lord Chard achieved his, by marrying her and retrieving the signet ring for his father.

All she felt they needed now was for Charlie to love her as deeply as she had come to love him.

Her reverie came to a sudden end when Tom put his hand up to halt the party. Was there trouble ahead? But he had only stopped to confer with Charlie.

Amy's stomach ceased churning as the party moved forward again, and any danger Tom had been cautious to avoid had turned out to be false, thank goodness!

It began to rain as they approached a village.

'We shall rest here,' announced Tom. 'But we must continue to be watchful and not cause any of the villagers to be attacked because we are here. We must not make our presence known in case Lenoir's men come here looking for us.'

Again, it was not a comfortable inn where he directed them to go — nor even a house, but a simple hay barn, with cattle nearby and cats chasing the rats.

'Sorry, ma'am, I am unable to offer you better accommodation,' Tom said as he came up to Amy and lifted her off her pony. 'Our safety has to be my priority. The brigands might come this way and be searching every village for us. This barn is dry and there is room for us and the horses. I'll go down into the village later and try and find some food for us.'

Molly had slipped off Lord Chard's mount and began to assist Amy into the barn with their bags, while Charlie saw to the horses.

Skippy had the best of it as he quickly made a cosy nest for himself in the hay, and flopped down on it, exhausted after his long day's run.

While Amy looked around fearfully, wondering what to do, Molly bustled about deciding where they should spend the night. Her cheerful banter made the barn almost as cosy as a tavern room.

Tom went in search of food and returned with what seemed like a feast for the famished travellers — freshly made bread, cheese, apples and a bottle of local wine — which enabled the men to relax and discuss their plans to get to Calais and onto the mail ship leaving for England tomorrow afternoon.

After eating, as the men relaxed enjoying their wine, Molly came up to

Amy to say, 'Come and let me help you prepared for bed.'

'We have only two beds,' Amy said, looking in consternation at the blankets Molly had arranged in the soft hay.

'That's right, ma'am,' chirped Molly. 'One is for me and Tom. You and your husband are to sleep the other side of the byre.' She giggled.

Understanding the maid's reasoning that the marital bed must be private, Amy smiled. Yet it was very far from the wedding night she had envisaged, in a large, carved wood bed with the finest cotton sheets and soft pillows!

She only knew that she was expected — and wanted — to sleep with her husband. And although feeling chilly and apprehensive, Amy's heart sang with joy.

But would Lord Charles Chard choose to sleep with her? Her husband had his precious signet ring back, and she had exchanged meaningful glances with him as they ate. It seemed to her they were no longer strangers, that they had developed a deeper understanding, an affectionate bond between them.

Had Lord Chard gone abroad by himself, he may not have been able to reclaim his ring — might even have been killed while trying to wrest it from the bandits. But his wife and her maid had come with him and they had enabled the deed to be done. He seemed to have changed his attitude towards the women now.

If they were caught and the bandits slaughtered them, Amy had the satisfaction of knowing she and Charlie would die with some true affection for each other, which made her glow inside and feel able to withstand the physical torment from the lack of the comfort and luxury she was having to endure.

She shivered at the thought of having any of her clothes removed in the freezing barn, and with only prickly hay to lie on — although she was tired and the smell of the hay was as delightful as any perfume.

Her true marriage was about to take

place. Charlie had already explained to her on her wedding night that their union would be at a time when they could be at peace and had the time to do so in comfort — which would not be tonight. Yet this night, she somehow sensed was the right time. Despite their poor surroundings, their exhaustion, and fear of being captured by the brigands, it seemed to be the time for them to fulfil his second promise made to his noble father — to marry and beget an heir.

Even if he was not in love with her, Amy knew Charlie respected her, and she was satisfied with that. It was warming and thrilling for Amy to allow herself to be engulfed by her natural desire to kiss her husband goodnight and lie next to him.

She slept until well past dawn.

⋆ ⋆ ⋆

On waking, Amy was aware that Charlie had gone, and that Molly's singing brightened the morning as the maid bustled about.

'Tom and I slept together last night,' Molly announced cheerfully with no hint of impropriety. 'It was lovely and warm.'

Amy could have said the same, but she refrained, as they were soon to be back in the constraints of English society. Herself being with child was one thing — having her maid pregnant too would be a completely different matter!

Molly had managed to procure a bowl of rain water to remove the soot from herself, and another for Amy to wash in. She had put out some clean underwear, and had sponged Amy's outer clothes ready for her to wear. Amy smiled her gratitude at her plucky little maid, who brushed the particles of straw out of her mistress's hair before she dressed it. If she did not yet have the skill of a hairdresser, at least it looked tidy.

Amy thought about how Molly had

bravely gone off by herself and found the ring, which made Amy determined that she would always stand by Molly when they returned to England, making sure that if her maid were indeed pregnant, she would not be without a decent living for her and her child.

Feeling more optimistic, Amy's thoughts dwelt on the journey back to England, although what faced her there was not her mother's home that she had known all her life. A new way of life as a Viscount's wife lay ahead of her, and it seemed daunting.

Now that she had tasted poverty, she had had enough of it already — and yet she did not look forward to wearing a tight corset with bone stays so that her figure would suit Regency ladies' fashions. Perhaps when she got home and was surrounded by women of fashion she would want to be like them, slipping on a clean chemise, a well-fitting corset, fresh drawers and petticoats under her dress . . . it certainly seemed preferable to the soiled and torn linen she had been obliged to wear up to now on their adventure. Every state in life had its drawbacks, she had to remember. That was one lesson she had learned from her trip abroad. And she had been largely lucky in her own station of life — despite having felt some dissatisfaction before she married.

Amy was determined, once she was home safely with Charlie, that she would be content with all she had — and perhaps also a child?

Before they moved to continue their journey down to the seaside, the men spent time deep in conversation, planning how to avoid capture and proceed with their escape — and they did not look too happy about it.

Charlie gave Amy a brief smile, but she could tell that his chief concern was to get her safely back to England.

How Amy would have relished a cup of coffee or hot chocolate! But such delights would have to wait, as once again she had to do as the men told her and continue with their ride, her muscles more sore than ever but her body refreshed for having washed and changed.

Autumn sea mists swirled around, giving the landscape an eerie cast as they set off on their horses, heading towards Calais harbour. It was a longer ride than Amy had expected, but by midday Tom was able to point out the packet ship already in the harbour.

The mood of their little party was almost cheerful with relief that at last their hazardous adventure was nearing its end. It was not, however, over. Amy noticed that Tom and Charlie were constantly alert to signs of being followed, of a possible attack by the brigands, turning in their saddles to look behind them, searching the landscape for signs of Lenoir's men.

At last, they ventured cautiously into the town of Calais. Immediately they all felt less exposed among the townsfolk. Day trippers from England were among the crowds in the port which made them less likely to stand out.

As it was too early for the ship to sail, they risked stopping at a quayside tavern for a meal. The horses were taken to the tavern's stables to be fed and rubbed down. Tom said he would have them returned to the stables they were hired from after the beasts had been fed and rested.

Amy noticed that even now neither Charlie nor Tom was at ease, constantly glancing around them as though they thought they might be observed and were being followed.

* * *

With more than three hours before the packet was due to depart and a similar interval until the passengers would be allowed on board, Charlie suggested the women took the dog for a stroll in the narrow streets of the seaside town to pass the time.

He came up close to Amy and solemnly instructed her, 'I pray you, do not get lost or delay boarding the ship.

The church clock will be visible from wherever you go. It will strike the hour.'

'I will not forget the time,' she assured him, as he put his hands on her shoulders as if trying to impress on her what he wanted her to do. 'I will watch the clock carefully.'

She looked up at him. Did her husband look agitated, distracted? Was he still seriously worried that the brigands may find them, even here at the port? Were there people in this town that might be on the lookout for them and would inform the brigands looking for them?

'Charlie,' she said, looking up candidly into his face, anxious to know that he too would be safe. 'What are you and Tom to do while we are walking in town? It seems obvious to me that have a reason for us to part this afternoon. Do you truly think is it possible that Lenoir and his men may have followed us here?'

His expression showed his anxiety, although his voice sounded confident.

'Yes, it is possible. Monsieur Lenoir has spies everywhere in this part of France and may yet track us down. As I have his means of income, he will be desperate to retake the signet ring. And we know of his tyrannical methods — his men will be cruel, brutal to anyone they catch with the ring.

'I will not risk anything happening to you women, so it is necessary for us to part for now. You and Molly can take the dog for a walk around the town shops and in the park here, before you go on board. Meanwhile, Tom and I will set up a wild goose chase for Lenoir and his men to follow and remove them from the quay area. It will enable you to embark the ship without me worrying about you.'

'But what about you, Charlie?'

Amy shuddered to think of what the French thugs might do to him, and her fear increased as she realised he and Tom might be seriously hurt or killed as the ring was snatched from them.

'Pray, do not worry! Tom and I will

make sure Lenoir does not steal my father's ring again! But should we find ourselves in danger, remember we are both soldiers and will be well able to evade him and any of his men who might be on our tail. The main thing is, I simply cannot have the worry of you women being caught with us.'

Amy shook herself free from his arms, walked a few paces from him, turned and said angrily, 'I care not for this plan for you to leave us. Surely there is no danger right here at port? Can we not go to a coffee house? We will not be noticed with the other passengers waiting to go on board.'

Charlie glared at her, making her afraid that he might become angry with her again.

'No, Amy, we cannot! Please do not argue with me. As I have already explained, any of these port traders and shopkeepers may be under Lenoir's control.

'During the French Revolution they stopped people at the borders from escaping, and some may still wish to gain a reward for exposing us. Now, Amy, I beg of you to do as I say! Promise me that you will go on board as soon as the boat crew allow passengers to go to their cabins. I have arranged a cabin and the ship's captain knows you may be boarding before me.'

Afraid to provoke another quarrel with him, when he already looked so careworn, Amy knew she must accept his decision for them to go their separate ways at least for a few hours, hard though it was for her to do so.

She recollected that were he still in the army, she might have had to send him off to battle. A soldier's wife had to accept that they must part at times, and that her husband could be injured.

Bravely, Amy looked up at his unshaven, worried face and said, 'I will do as you ask, husband. I promise to board the ship on time — and you must promise to take care of yourself, Charlie.'

His smile was slight but she could tell

that he was relieved that she agreed to do as he told her.

Cartloads of mail sacks were arriving at the quay, and the shouts of the drivers and porters caused Amy to look around.

When Charlie grasped her hands firmly and looked deeply into her eyes he said in a commanding voice, 'It is essential for you to obey me, Amy. I want you to promise me again that when the town clock strikes three you will go forthwith to the ship and get on board immediately — even if you do not see me. The captain will be expecting you and has already taken your travel bags on board.'

Although she had defied him on two occasions — first about bringing Molly, and then about bringing her dog — Amy had no doubt in her mind that this time he was deadly serious that she should obey him as a wife should obey her husband.

She was truly married to him now, and she loved him and admired him.

She must also learn to trust him, even if she felt the urge to argue that she would not sail away and leave him behind.

'I promise,' she said with a heavy heart.

He held her face gently in his two hands and bent down to kiss her lips tenderly. Then he gave her one of his endearing smiles.

So it was agreed, and as they parted Amy felt a sharp pang of loss.

So little time had passed since they had first met and decided to abandon the normal rituals and correct procedure for their marriage. They had both jumped into the unknown, but in their case she felt with renewed confidence that it was the right thing for them to do. Amy would never regret her unusual marriage.

Having consented to part temporarily from the menfolk, while waiting for the ship to sail, she would pass the time by looking at the town's shops, perhaps buying a souvenir with the money Charlie had given her.

Molly seemed confident that Tom could look after himself and Charlie, and was happy to walk the dog in the fresh air until three o'clock.

Amy was fascinated by everything she saw in the little coastal town of Callais and it helped to make the time pass by more quickly.

When the church clock chimed — One . . . Two . . . Three . . . — the two women hurried back to the ship and waited by the gangplank for their men.

'Lord Chard said we were to go aboard, Molly. We can find our cabin and then we can return and wait by the gangplank so that Charlie and Tom can see we are on board.'

Time went by quickly as they stood watching other passengers board, chattering happily about their day trip. Soon the last of mail bags were being hoisted on deck, and the sailors began casting off, ready to set sail.

Amy began to feel a dreadful cold sweat when Charlie and Tom did not appear and it became clear to her that the packet ship was preparing to sail without them!

'Where are they?' she cried, looking along the quay, desperate to catch sight of them.

10

When the men still had not arrived by the time the sailors were ready to sail the ferry away from France, Amy began to feel tortured.

Why had Charlie not come? Had he and Tom been caught by Lenoir's ruffians?

She wanted to leave the ship and search for him — but had he not made her promise that she would sail when the ship left?

Of all the deprivations she had suffered on her 'honeymoon', this was the worst — to lose the man she had come to love and genuinely wanted to live with for the rest of her life.

Even cheerful little Molly had no words of comfort as the minutes ticked by, but then Amy thought that was because her maid had formed a strong attachment for Tom, and was suffering as much she was, wondering what had happened to their lovers.

As Amy and her maid stood patiently waiting by the gangplank, their eyes searching for any sight of their menfolk, the time for the ship's departure came. At any moment, Amy expected to be ordered by the Captain to get out of the way, or get off his ship!

Seagulls flew and cried around the departing ship. The last-minute bustle of the passengers and their chatter as they settled themselves for the sea voyage contrasted with the silence of the two waiting women. The crew's seamanship began to take over from the harbour workers' tasks in a well-practised exercise to depart the harbour.

'Dunno what could have happened to 'em, ma'am,' Molly said, shrugging her shoulders.

Almost breathless with worry, Amy asked, 'What shall we do if they do not come?'

'I honestly dunno what we should do, ma'am.'

Amy knew her maid was only expressing her dismay as the minutes before the mail packet departure ran out.

Should they get off the ship, or sail to England without Charlie and Tom?

A sailor hauling in the gang plank gave her a rough shove, while another yelled at Molly, who held Skippy in her arms, 'Get that dog below! Or it'll fall overboard.'

Protesting was useless. Both women looked unkempt, poorly dressed, and had no right to delay the packet mail from sailing on time.

Tears formed in Amy's eyes as she again remembered her promise — Charlie had insisted that she leave France on this ferry. Perhaps he would sail on the next one? How hard it was for her to keep that promise, to trust him.

Amy longed to jump off the ship, but she must not. Charlie had been most insistent that she sail to England without him if he did not turn up. He had given her no reason why this might happen, and a cold fear overcame her to think that he perhaps knew the bandits would catch up with them, looking for his ring, and that he wanted to make sure the women were safe, no matter what happened to him.

The captain's ruddy face showed his concern for them as he approached them.

'I'm sorry your menfolk have missed the boat, but we have to set sail, ma'am,' he told them. 'The tide won't wait.'

The wind was flapping the sails that had been hoisted, the seamen were pattering about the deck catching the ropes from the ship's last moorings, and stashing them away neatly. The deck moved as the waves rocked it and the heavy gangplank was hauled back into the ship with much yelling from the crew.

Amy felt sick at heart.

She had spent the first few days of her married life on a quest that had been unpleasant at times but successful.

Yet now it seemed that at the last moment it had partially failed, because she had lost the man she had come to love.

Viscount Charles Chard had made sure his wife was going to be safe. She would go back to England and claim her status and an easy life as his wife — but without what she wanted most of all . . . him.

How cruel life could be, Amy thought as tears streamed down her face.

Lord Chard had survived the battle at Waterloo, overcome his injuries, and might yet sire an heir if he survived. In fact, Amy might even now already be carrying his child.

Molly was very quiet. Amy wondered whether she too was facing up to the prospect of having lost the man she loved.

With a final jerk the ship was free of the harbour and set off to sail the wide sea. In her misery, Amy barely heard the sound of the rigging being battered in the wind and the shouts of the crew as the ship slowly headed out into the English Channel, where the waves could toss the ship about mercilessly.

For the first half hour Amy refused go down to the little cabin they had been allotted, but stood on deck holding onto a spar for support, looking at the harbour wall becoming smaller as the ship eased away from it.

Her heart heavy with sorrow, she fought back her tears. After all, she had no proof that any harm had come to Charlie or Tom, or that he might not take a later sailing if for some reason they had been delayed.

Yet what if some of the brigands had caught up with them? Although, being soldiers, they might well manage to evade capture and be in hiding somewhere. Banishing any thought of the possible cruel treatment they might suffer if they had been caught — and the ring found and wrested once again from Charlie — Amy could only pray that at least he would not be killed.

Lord Chard had made sure that she and Molly were going safely back to England, so whatever had occurred she hoped Charlie had made similar arrangements to save himself from harm, even if the brigands caught had them. She could not bear the thought that he would have lost his father's signet ring again! All that suffering they had endured would have been in vain!

Dejectedly, she turned and went down to her cabin. She still had to think of her maid, and the responsibility she had for her.

★ ★ ★

After Viscount Charles Chard and Tom Brown left the women earlier to wander around the old town of Calais among the local people and the day trippers from England waiting to board the ferry and return home, they felt satisfied that their women would be well shielded from Lenoir's men in the crowd.

They had impressed upon the women

the need to board the ship well before it set sail. The captain of the vessel had been given their sailing papers and had paid for passage and a cabin.

Foremost in Charlie's mind was not, as Amy thought, that he was protecting her because she might be able to give him an heir, but because he had come to realise he did not want to lose her.

He admired her common sense and and her pluckiness, and this realisation came as a shock to him because he had presumed he never would want female companionship. He had merely, he thought, done his duty, married an older girl, not a beauty, but an agreeable female.

However, he now felt glad that he had. Amy was no young, docile maiden, but he was pleased about that too. Having a woman who would challenge him, who was able to cope with difficult situations, and proved a friendly lover was far better than Lord Charles Chard ever hoped for.

Tom, able scout that he was, was concentrating on the possible dangers they may still face and had spotted a number of uncouth-looking riders following them, now that they had parted from the women. He told Charlie what he had observed in the distance.

'I'd not be surprised if they are Lenoir's thugs,' Tom said pointing to the horses and riders. 'We must prevent them getting into town.'

They immediately went to the stables to hire a couple of hunters — horses that could withstand a hard ride.

Charlie frowned. 'Do not forget my injured leg, Tom. I cannot ride so well as you, and fear I am already in considerable discomfort from our long days of riding.'

'I have that in mind, Captain Chard,' replied Tom with a grin.

Without appearing to be in a hurry, so as not to attract attention, the two men rode out of Calais.

Suddenly Tom reined in his horse and asked, 'Can you see that party of riders over there?' He pointed towards the top of a hill opposite the one they had reached. Although a sea mist shrouded their view to some extent, Charlie could make out five or six riders about to descend into the town.

'Lenoir's men?' he questioned nervously.

'Aye,' Tom replied, 'I'm sure they are.'

Both men watched the group galloping towards the harbour only a mile away.

Charlie felt sweat form on his brow.

Tom's horse was ready to chase after them as it snorted and circled around.

'You must stay out of sight, m'lord. You're not able to ride, twist and turn on horseback and jump your horse, as I am. Stay hidden,' Tom shouted. 'I'll attract their attention, so they will follow me away from the town. That will prevent them from going down to the harbour and finding the women before the ferry departs.'

'Very well, Tom, but take care!'

Abruptly Tom cantered off, yelling back to Charlie, 'Remain on your horse but behind those bushes. Be ready to come out of cover and follow me when I return.'

Charlie knew he could no longer ride as skilfully as Tom, so he had no choice but to wait, hidden by the undergrowth, while Tom led the brigands on a goose chase. He had to chuckle as he watched his friend attract the thugs' attention, then pretend to race away from them, so they followed him. It was a game to Tom — but a dangerous game.

Charlie was glad he had a pistol under his coat. Although he was not able to assist Tom playing the fox to be hunted, he was a crack shot with a gun — which may yet prove to be useful.

As he waited, Charlie now had time to think about his life. Being born into the landed gentry, he had always been able to enjoy whatever took his fancy. He had happily skimmed through the pleasantries of being young, able to do as he pleased. He had even fallen in love — and out again just as swiftly — several times in his youth.

But now he was seriously deep into considering his life ahead, burdened with responsibilities. Not that it entirely daunted him to become aware of the challenges ahead . . . that was, if he even made it home to England.

He wished he could be of use to Tom, who had done so much for him in the past couple of years.

After what seemed like an age, Charlie startled on hearing his name called, and Tom came into view on his sweating horse.

Charlie prodded his heels into his horse's flanks to urge the animal to emerge from his hiding place and moved his pistol, ready to use.

'Follow me. We'll make for the next coastal village,' Tom shouted at him. 'And put that bloody pistol away! We don't want anyone to suspect us of being involved with Lenoir's brigands.'

They set off at a steady pace, in single file, so they could be watchful for a sighting of the enemy while they rode, discussing their next move.

Charlie realised that their opportunity to catch the mail boat in Calais had gone and it was now impossible for them to get back to the port of Calais and join the women on board the ferry by three o'clock.

Charlie prayed that Amy would obey him and sail anyway, as he had told her to.

It certainly helped that Tom was familiar with the coastal area. He was able to guide Charlie along narrow cliff paths and sheep tracks which, they hoped, the brigands would not know of.

The tiny bay they came to was deserted. No fisher folk were living there.

'Follow me,' Tom said as he dismounted.

Leaving the horses, they slid down the hill towards the sandy beach. They were not keen to remain long in the area now they were hunted men. Concealed in the sand dunes was a small craft, obviously belonging to someone who used it to go fishing.

Charlie was horrified to see Tom untying the row boat as if he owned it.

'You must escape from France,' Tom hissed. 'Don't just stand there, m'lord. Leave the horses to graze and find water in a brook. Help me drag the boat down the beach into the sea.'

'We cannot simply take it, Tom,' Charlie protested.

'Worry not, I shall bring this borrowed fisherman's boat back, I know it is important for his livelihood.' He gasped for breath as his energy was diverted into hauling the craft from its hiding place. 'And I shall return the horses to the tavern we hired them from — once I have seen you off safely.'

The two men huffed and puffed to slide the boat over the sand and into the rippling waves. There Tom leaped into the boat, found the oars under the seat, and after seating himself on the craft, which was now afloat, he helped Charles on board and began to row out towards the bigger waves into the sea.

'Lenoir's men will be here searching

for me very soon — they were on my tail. When they see us sail away they'll leave, thinking there's no hope of them getting the ring back.'

11

A little way off the French coast, the packet ship seemed to suddenly stop. It still rocked on the waves and Amy, who lay on her bunk, would not have noticed it had Molly not done so.

'We ain't off the French coast yet, ma'am,' Molly said, looking out of the porthole. 'But the ship ain't moving no more neither.'

Amy, deep in misery, was not interested in how long the ship took to reach Dover. As far as she was concerned, it was a tragedy that her trip to accompany her husband to reclaim his father's valuable signet ring, was so bittersweet. Lord Charles had his father's ring, yes — but only to find he had unleashed a pack of wolves after him!

She realised how much she missed Charlie, how much he meant to her.

He had not made a fuss over her

during the trip — he had even largely ignored her, and they had their disagreements — but nevertheless, their relationship had deepened, and Amy felt that a firm bond had been forged between them.

Of course, they had also become lovers, so her honeymoon had been successful in that respect — but the quest to bring back the signet ring seemed more akin to a disaster, as she knew not what had befallen the ring — or Charlie.

She feared for him, unable to stop her thoughts straying to tales of how brutal bandits could be. Charlie had been ill, recovering from his wounds at Waterloo. He was no longer a fit, young man, able to shake off a second beating. Amy shuddered to think of his condition at that moment, of any suffering he may be going through.

If those thieves took his ring away once more, he would be as badly off as he had been when he first set out to find it.

How would he manage to stop the debts that would be piling up and might soon cripple his father financially? She felt sure the Earl of Collingwood would be able to eventually let it be widely known that his ring was no longer in his possession, and that it could no longer be used for him to honour any promise to pay drafts with the seal upon it. But how long would that take?

She was not afraid of the prospect that they may have to live on a much reduced income — she had already accepted that a modest life would be her fate before Lord Chard came to her home and asked her to marry him.

No, she was worried about what had happened to Charlie because she had come to truly love him. Would she ever see him again? How fervently she prayed that he would be safe. And Tom too, who had done so much to help them locate the ring.

Where was it now? Where was Charlie?

*   *   *

Drained, physically and emotionally, Amy finally fell asleep, until loud banging on the cabin door woke her with a start.

Molly rushed to open it and from across the room, Amy heard her shriek, 'Crikey! Lord Chard! You're drippin' wet!'

Half asleep when the hammering on the door started, Amy gasped. Was she dreaming? Raising herself up on her elbow she peered across the gloom of the cabin towards the door and saw a large figure pushing inside the cabin.

A reasuringly familiar voice boomed out, 'Don't stand gawping at me, Molly! Find me a towel.'

Amy leaped from her bunk — Charlie had come back to her!

She rushed to fetch a towel even before Molly could do so, running to help dry him.

'Charlie. You are safe! Oh, thank God!'

'As may be, but I'm d-damned c-c-cold,' he stuttered, his teeth physically chattering.

Molly, observing that Charlie seemed to be alone, rushed out of the cabin to seek Tom, leaving Amy to dry her shivering husband.

Whether it was raining outside, or he had been drenched by the sea spray, Amy guessed that he had been picked up from a small boat at sea. She felt too overwhelmed with relief to have him safely back with her to worry him about how he had managed to board the ferry.

'Where's the dog?' Charlie asked several times as she helped him to remove his sopping wet garments. She picked up his soaked waistcoat, and searched the pocket for the signet ring, but could not find it.

'Where is your ring?' she asked fearfully. Had the brigands caught him and stolen the ring?

With only her paisley shawl to drape over him after he had peeled off his wet clothes, she looked in her bag for something for him to wear, but all he seemed interested in was Skippy — whom Amy assured him was down near the cargo rooms, curled up with some mail sacks for warmth.

'I must see Skippy,' Charlie said, giving his hair a final rub with the damp towel.

Molly barged in, grinning and carrying a pile of old sailors' clothes.

''Ere you are, m'lord. Dry togs for you to wear until you get back to England and your valet can get you dressed all proper like.'

She turned to explain to Amy, 'I found out that Tom went back to France in the rowing boat 'e'd borrowed to bring Lord Chard out to catch the packet ship. He wanted to return the boat 'e'd borrowed, and 'ad to water the horses they'd left on the beach and take them back to Calais.'

'Go and get Skippy,' Charlie ordered distractedly as Amy selected a sailor's jersey and breeches for him to wear.

Molly said, 'You need have no care

about him, my lord, he's fast asleep in the warm supply room.'

'Then go and fetch him!' Charlie shouted — and then sneezed.

Was Charlie suffering from some sort of fever that the cold sea drenching had given him? Amy frowned. Why was he so insistent that he should see the dog? He did not like dogs — had not wanted her dog to come with them when he left England. So why was he so anxious about Skippy's welfare now — even though he had become his master and the dog obeyed him now?

'You had better go and fetch Skippy,' Amy whispered to Molly. 'Humour him — he may be suffering from some disorder of the brain after his dousing in the sea!'

Amy persuaded Charlie to sit on her bunk and refrained from laughing at his odd appearance. Not that she was much better dressed, after her days of trekking and camping ordeals.

When Molly had gone, the ship began rolling in the giant Channel waves. Amy went to sit close by Charlie and was gratified that he hugged her close to him.

'Amy, Amy . . . you are a truly wonderful wife.'

Still thinking he was suffering from the strain he had been under, she did not question him, but simply cuddled into to him to keep him warm.

A knock on the door was followed by a sailor boy who came in bearing a cup of chocolate, saying, 'With the Captain's compliments, sir,' as he handed the hot drink to Lord Chard.

Then Skippy's bark could be heard. Amy quickly removed the drinking cup from Charlie's hands as Skippy came bounding into the cabin and seemed to want to lick his lordship all over!

Charlie ordered, 'Be quiet. Sit.' Then he felt under the dog's fur and unbuckled the collar. Then he handed the collar to Amy . . .

Her hand immediately went to her mouth to stifle a cry when she saw something glitter. The signet ring had been threaded onto the dog's collar!

Neither she nor Molly had even noticed it, although Charlie must have put it there before he had left them in Calais.

Flabbergasted, and delighted to see the ring safe, Amy laughed and cried at the same time.

'Well, fancy that!' exclaimed Molly. 'I never noticed the ring right under me nose all the while I was walking Skippy around Calais!'

Unbeknown to him, Skippy had been the keeper of the ring all along during those tense hours when they were being pursued for it. Lord Charles had cleverly hidden the ring on the dog knowing Amy would keep the animal — and therefore the ring — safe. Had the brigands caught and threatened her husband, they would have been unable to find the ring on either of the men.

His lordship's lips twitched with a smile as he placed the signet ring on his finger, muttering to himself, 'The next time I take this off it will be when I hand it back to my papa — and mighty glad I shall be to do so!'

Now that the signet ring was back in his possession, Charlie breathed a deep sigh of relief. Then, in a state of exhaustion, he lay back on the bunk and was almost immediately fast asleep — while his wife Amy lay close by his side to keep him warm.

★   ★   ★

The ship arrived back in Dover without mishap and after the mail was unloaded and the passengers disembarked, the Captain was able to hire a carriage for his odd-looking nobleman passenger, who had paid him well for his delay on the French coast to pick him up en route.

Amy was exceedingly relieved that her adventurous honeymoon holiday was over and she was back safely in her homeland.

She had achieved what she had wished. She had been abroad and seen what life was like on the Continent. Apart from suffering from discomfort and fatigue, no great harm had come to them. She had come to know the man she had married in haste and now knew that she and her husband would be happy living together.

Yet the state she was in — her clothes, her hair and her general appearance — was little better than a pauper, and her noble husband looked similarly unlordly in his well-worn sailor's clothes!

In England, where these kind of things mattered, where appearance was everything, they were going to be the laughing stock of civilised society, and she had no chance now of being accepted by the ton.

Lord Chard, however, had been thinking about what to do when they arrived in England in the early morning.

'We are to go to my Aunt Matilda's,' he informed Amy as he climbed into the old carriage he had managed to hire, with their small amount of luggage, chatty maid and dog already inside.

As the carriage moved forward he went on to explain, 'She is my father's sister, an eccentric old lady, somewhat forthright in her opinions, but she has been a favourite aunt of mine since childhood. She lives nearby.'

Amy would have much preferred to go to a tavern to wash and tidy herself before she could possibly present herself to any of her husband's relations. Charlie, she realised, would probably feel the same — a nobleman, as he was, would not enjoy being so roughly dressed. However, she was sure he had in mind to rectify the situation as soon as possible — and no one would expect to see finely attired people emerge from the ramshackle old coach they were in.

The coach took them towards Royal Tunbridge Wells, and Amy's heart sank even further, for they were heading to one of the most fashionable spas. It would be the death of her social life were she to be seen in her present ragged condition! Oh, why had he not taken them to an inn where they could have at least tidied themselves a little!

As Charlie seemed to be suffering, exhausted physically and mentally, after his escape from France, and deep in his thoughts, Amy did not like to question him further about the destination he had in mind. While he did not appear too dreadfully ill, he looked utterly exhausted — as she was herself.

No conversation took place as they were bounced along in the old carriage. After all, Amy now thought, it ought to be of no real consequence, and merely being with him was comfort enough.

She looked down at the signet ring now on his finger and thought bitterly of the trouble it had caused them. But, had it? Perhaps, had his father not given it to him the talisman ring he might have been killed at Waterloo.

Then, if it had not been stolen and he had not had to retrieve it she would not have had her honeymoon holiday adventure, testing though it had been at times. She now had something to look back on and remember, and could now laugh at their experiences. Even when sometimes things had gone awry, they were lucky enough to avoid any real danger.

As for not being accepted by polite society, as far as Amy was concerned she had not, just a few months ago, ever expected to be anyway. She had never aspired to be a social climber.

She now recognised that she would be expected to socialise with people in high society occasionally, and must try and make her husband proud of her looks, and appear at ease in aristocratic company. She had a responsibility to bring up any children they might have to fit into that top class of society too.

By going to France with her husband they had formed a bond, and were comfortable together. She felt he had every intention to do as he said he would, to respect her and look after her.

Perhaps he would always remain some-what remote from her simply because that was his nature. Boys, especially noble ones, were brought up to hide their feelings. Harsh schooling and domineering fathers were what little boys expected, preparing them for their future duties as noblemen with responsibilities.

She was beginning to understand Charlie was very loyal, putting his sense of duty towards his parents, his wife and friends, before his desires. Also, he was past the first flush of youth, had reached maturity and had the right to order his own life, not being burdened by what others thought he ought to do.

Amy was determined not to add to his burden by demanding he do this, or that, simply to please her. Nevertheless, she felt embarrassed to be in her present ragged state.

Her thoughts were abruptly cut off by Charlie's voice saying, 'Amy, I am sorry to have to tell you this, but when I place you under my aunt's protection I must leave you for some time.'

Charlie had opened his eyes to look at his wife apologetically. Amy gasped.

Was he going to leave her — again?

He put up a hand as if to bat off protestations.

'I know, I know . . . and you have every right to complain of it, but I assure you it is necessary for me to go forthwith to London to sort out our finances — or I fear we risk losing everything.'

Swallowing her protest, Amy closed her eyes and bowed her head. She had to accept his decision.

To him it was essential he returned his father's ring to him and halted forthwith the payments being made to Monsieur Lenoir. She swallowed and managed to say in a steady voice, 'I realise you must take your father's ring to your bank and save what remains of his fortune.'

His body leaned forward as his large, warm hand came to rest over hers. It was a rough-skinned hand, though it was heartwarming to her.

He cleared his throat awkwardly.

'When I asked you to marry me, this

was not the way I had expected, or wanted, our marriage to be, I fear.'

Comforted by his touch, Amy looked up, her eyes melting into his.

'Of course you did not — no more than I — but I am not complaining. Indeed it was I who asked you to take me abroad — demanded it, even.'

He chuckled. 'I fear you got more discomfort and trouble than you bargained for! I did not think it would take so long, or be so difficult, to retrieve Papa's signet ring.'

'He should not have given it to you!' Amy blurted out.

Charlie shifted in his seat.

'Perhaps not, but I think he meant well. In truth, what happened to it was unforeseen. It was ill luck that it landed in a brigand's hands who was able to use it for robbery.'

Amy had to concede that was so. Guilty that she had made him feel embarrassed about his wretched position, she said, 'Charlie, I married you for richer or poorer. You must know that even if you are not successful and we have a life of hardship ahead of us, I shall stand by you.'

'I thank you for saying so.'

He moved further forward so that his lips touched hers, gently, briefly.

Then he eased himself back into the carriage seat and, after a long sigh, he slept awhile again.

Amy smiled fondly at him.

He was not the bravest of men — for after all, it had been Tom and Molly who had shown the courage to retrieve the signet ring. Charlie had yet to do his part in restoring his father's ring and securing his fortune. She had to give him time, had to continue being patient. Her trials were not over yet, and her good behaviour was crucial.

Even the thought of having to fit into a higher society than she was used to being in filled her with dread, with perhaps more discomfort and humiliations ahead of her.

Yet her heart sang with hope that their future would be rosier when all

their troubles were behind them . . .
eventually . . .

* * *

What Viscount Chard and his lady did
not know at that time was that Tom
Brown, their scout during their adventures in France, was in serious trouble.

After rowing the boat that had taken
the viscount to the packet ship to get
him back to England safely, Tom dragged
the borrowed boat back to the bay he
had taken it from — and was immediately surrounded and captured by the
party of French brigands who had been
chasing him earlier that day, furious that
Tom had evaded them. Lenoir's men
had been able to see him rowing out to
sea and the mail ship waiting for the
viscount. On Tom's return to the beach,
they swooped on him.

Tom had expected to return the
borrowed boat to where its owner had
left it tied up without too much
difficulty. He used all his strength to

row away from the ferry ship in the choppy sea, after the crew had put down nets and helped Lord Chard to climb up into their ship. The forceful wind and roar of the sea had prevented any goodbyes being heard as Charlie and Tom parted.

Tom managed to manoeuvre the small fishing craft back into the calmer waters of the bay. There he planned to collect and return the horses to the stables they had hired them from in Calais, before finding a tavern to sleep for the night.

He had not truly given a thought to the possibility that Lenoir's men would lie in wait for him when he returned to France. They had been fooled by Tom leading them a merry dance before he had collected Charlie, and they had both rowed off into the ocean to put Lord Chard safely on board the ferry ship. Although they were not able to prevent Charlie, who they presumed had the signet ring, from escaping, they rubbed their hands with glee to observe

Tom coming back with the boat he had borrowed.

The brigands hid in the tall sand dune grasses so Tom could not see them, and pounced on him as soon as he began dragging the boat back to its mooring. Caught by the tough, surly Frenchmen, who were ready to butcher him, he cried out that if they wanted the signet ring, only he knew where it was now, and how they could obtain it.

As their livelihoods depended on the things the ring bought them, the brigands stayed their hands and agreed to allow Tom to take them across the channel immediately to search for the ring.

'Monsieur Lenoir bought the ring at Lille Market, it belongs to him,' the oafish robbers shouted at Tom, ignoring the fact that the ring was being used illegally.

Finding himself in danger of being battered to death, and knowing that if they killed him they might still seek to find and kill Viscount Chard or his father, Tom could only think that he must bargain with the villains.

'Only I can show you where to go to find the ring in England,' he lisped through his split lip and bloodied nose.

One brigand said, 'Maybe he's right. Monsieur Lenoir won't thank us for letting the ring slip through our fingers.'

The rest of the mob agreed. One gave Tom a savage kick and spat out, 'I say let's steal a fishing boat from the village harbour and take ourselves and our horses over the Channel and make this Englishman show us where it is.'

Shuddering at the thought of what torture and death might lie ahead for him, Tom was tempted to give up and simply allow the brigands to execute him — but then he thought of Molly.

Molly, the brave little maid who had risked her life climbing up and down the chateau flues to get the signet ring. Molly with her impish smile and indomitable spirit. Tom had planned, when he returned to England, to ask Molly to marry him.

Tom also realised that if the brigands took him back to England, he might yet have a chance to escape them.

12

Although relieved to be back in England, Amy felt exhausted after enduring so much worry in the hour or so before Charlie had returned. Delighted too, discovering how he had hidden the signet ring on Skippy's collar, she hoped that life would soon become easier for both of them.

At present it was not.

She was being taken to his aunt's house which was near the coast. She hated the thought of having to meet this aunt of his in her present state. What manner of person was the noblewoman? Surely she would object to having her nephew turn up late in the evening, looking as though he had been thrown out of prison — and with a wife she knew nothing of, looking frightful too?

Before long the squeaky carriage

slowed and the coachman turned the horses to enter a drive, with a lodge keeper who came out to open the gates for the visitors. Soon they stopped in front of a great house, and before Amy had dismounted, a butler opened the front door to greet them.

'Good day, Martin. Is my aunt at home?'

The well-trained butler, Martin, did not give so much as a hint that he had even noticed Charlie's sailor's outfit, let alone disapproved of it.

'I will inform her ladyship that you have come, my lord,' he said with a bow, as if the nobleman was dressed exquisitely as a man of fashion.

It soon became apparent to Amy why the uninvited nephew and new wife were not unwelcome, for Aunt Matilda, although an educated lady, was well beyond the age of wondering what others thought of her! She was a rich widow, able to enjoy her life as she saw fit. She had a well-run house with devoted servants. She had no reason to worry now of an invasion by Napoleon as he had been carted off to some remote island, and her brave nephew had done his duty in fighting at Waterloo to put him there.

After the butler returned, with the message that they were to come in, Amy stepped out of the carriage, and took Charlie's arm to enter the house.

In the hall, several female servants had assembled, curious to see the unexpected visitors and to assist the party inside. Amy noticed some of the women looked amazed to see their state of dress — a younger maid tittered to another — but none of them refused to perform their duties.

A few recognised the Viscount Chard they had known for years when he visited his aunt, and of whom they had been very fond. Molly was taken to the kitchens while Lord Chard and his wife were escorted to meet their hostess.

Aunt Matilda was seated in her break-fast parlour like a queen on a throne. She seemed pleased to see her nephew and looked quizzically at his bride.

'Been to a fancy dress ball, have you?' she asked with a twinkle in her eyes.

Charlie stepped forward and kissed her cheek.

'No, aunt. We have suffered a rough crossing from France, where we went for our honeymoon,' he explained.

Aunt Matilda reached for her quizzing glass and looked them both up and down.

'You don't have to tell me you have been through the mill! I can see it for m'self! Escaped from the Bastille by the looks of it! I've heard the French mob have been treating some of their nobles cruelly — their King and Queen included, and their children . . . poor little prince and princess.'

'The Revolution was some time ago, aunt.'

'Well!' the elderly lady declared. 'So, what happened to you over there?'

'That I will explain to you shortly. In the meantime let me introduce you to my wife, Amy.'

'Come nearer, my dear.'

Aunt Matilda held out her hand for Amy to take as Amy had been afraid to come to close to the lady in case her unwashed clothes stank.

'You may kiss me, Amy.'

She was relieved to find the old lady did not think Amy beneath her. Matilda wore a morning dress that would not have looked out of place in a theatre, and even an exotic headdress covered her thinning hair. Obviously, she was content to be an unusual old lady, enjoying a comfortable life in her own way.

Amy curtsied, aware that she was being well scrutinised.

'Hmm . . . ' Matilda murmured after she had finished her examination.

She turned to Charlie saying, 'I heard about Harriet's wedding to Horatio, but not that you had found yourself a bride. It was a rather precipitous decision, then?'

'It was, aunt, but none the worse for that. Amy has proved her mettle admirably.'

'Well, Charlie, she may look beautiful in your eyes, but she looks as if she urgently needs the attention of my servants to dress her properly.'

'As do I, aunt. Please excuse our poor manner of dress — and lack of manners with our sudden intrusion. We were caught up in an unfortunate adventure in France.'

Matilda's eyes gleamed. 'I can well believe you have been up to something. I warrant I'll be most interested to hear all about it — when you are looking more respectable.'

'My dear aunt.' Charlie stepped forward, bowed in a lordly fashion, and said, 'I shan't kiss you in my present state, but if you permit me to bathe and dress, I shall certainly do so then!'

Aunt Matilda gave a chuckle. 'I shan't object to that! Give the bell pull a tug, Charlie.'

The butler entered the room and was instructed to tell the maids to prepare to help bathe the visitors, and to find some gentleman's clothes for the viscount and a dress for his lady.

'And bring in some coffee — and a little breakfast, I venture, for they look half starved!'

The butler was about to leave when Amy asked, 'May I ask that my maid, Molly, is given something to eat?'

The butler replied stiffly, 'Ma'am, your young maid Molly is not backward in coming forward and has already made herself at home in the servants' kitchen. She has made your little dog comfortable, too, my lady.'

Charlie looked at Amy and grimaced, then turned to his aunt.

'Aunt, please excuse the maid's lack of decorum. She was given to my wife as a temporary help when we were in a hurry before going to France, and she is untrained. However, I assure you she is trustworthy. She may be a little uncouth in her manners, but she is, in fact, very courageous — as I will explain when I tell you about our adventures.'

'Indeed,' his aunt said, smiling. 'I am

intrigued to hear all about your . . . honeymoon.' She picked at the breakfst dishes before her. 'Now, I will not permit you to sit down to breakfast with me while you both look beyond respectability. Your breakfast will be taken up to your rooms on trays, after you have bathed and changed.'

The butler hid a grin as he left to give the servants their instructions. His life was somewhat tedious at times with only an old lady to serve. This unexpected intrusion into the house was a welcome entertainment for all the staff, who were not finding the extra work they had been landed with a nuisance. Even Skippy had managed to garner many strokes and cuddles, as well as last night's scraps to eat.

★ ★ ★

Amy was escorted upstairs to a guest room to be given over to maids for their expert ministrations.

Charlie, too, was whisked upstairs to

be washed, shaved and transformed from a rough-looking seaman into the gentleman he was.

The maid helping Amy to wash her hair announced, 'I can't understand why your little maid was so sooty, ma'am!'

Not knowing what Molly had offered as an excuse, Amy avoided saying anything about her climb up and down the chateau chimney. She was merely pleased to hear that Molly had been able to bathe and wash her hair.

A little later, quiet but insistent knocks on the door made Amy start.

Relaxing in the bathtub and having her hair dried and brushed, Amy was annoyed to be disturbed, wanting only to lie down in peace.

'It is I,' her husband murmured as Amy hurriedly stepped out of the tub and wrapped a gown around her nakedness.

Charlie, clad in gentlemen's riding clothes, slipped into the room. Not dressed in the height of fashion, in clothes that did not fit him well, he at least looked presentable. No, more than that — he looked as a well-dressed gentleman should and his looks did him credit.

Amy could not understand why a younger woman had not snapped him up as a husband some time ago. She supposed, either he had not met the woman he wanted, or he could enjoy their company without the responsibility of marriage.

'I must leave for London immediately,' he told his wife directly, hating to hurt her again.

Amy gasped. 'Surely not — already?'

He drew himself up and nodded.

'Yes, I must ride to London today. It will be the quickest way for me to see the bank manager and stop these illegal payments.'

She almost cried out, No, you cannot leave me stranded here with your formidable aunt and with no clothes or money! Yet she knew he had to get to his father's bank as soon as he could.

She closed her eyes while she strove to control her feelings and not give into righteous indignation that she was to be left again.

Of course, she realised he had to go — and she had to be brave and let him do so.

As he stepped forward to kiss her wet cheek, she longed to lock her arms around him to prevent him from leaving her. She did not know why, but some premonition of danger dismayed her.

Charlie's aunt was not pleased either to find her nephew wishing to dash away so soon after he had arrived. Still, made of sterner stuff than most women, she was able to control her emotions and promise graciously to look after Amy until his return.

Privately Matilda thought she detected an admirable new sense of responsibility in her young nephew, which pleased her.

Bidding his aunt farewell, leaving an allowance for Amy to spend as she wished, he kissed her tenderly and promised to return as soon as possible. Having his aunt's permission to ask her old groom to select the best horse for riding with his sore leg, Charlie set off on the London Road.

★ ★ ★

'Allow me to accompany you to the London Road, m'lord,' the groom had offered.

'No, thank you. It is easy enough to find and I shall leave my aunt's horse at the posting inn and catch the early evening coach into London.'

Charlie swung painfully into the saddle, nodded to the stable boy and groom and set off at a fast gallop.

Perturbed to find the daylight fading already as the autumn wind whipped up, shaking the last of the leaves off the trees which swirled around his horse's cantering hooves, Charlie was pleased to think that this first part of his journey, in the desolate countryside from his aunt's house to the London

Road, would soon be over.

How he wished he had not had to leave his wife so abruptly, but it was urgent for him to settle business with the signet ring without delay.

He had concealed the ring in the tassel of his boot — out of sight because it was so obviously valuable. At present, Charlie was not dressed in the finest of clothes a nobleman might wear, and it might make people wonder why he was wearing such an obviously expensive ring.

Missing Tom, who had been his riding companion and his excellent scout and advisor, Charlie realised he had embarked on the most daunting task he had ever faced in his life. For once he was on his own, having to make his own decisions and not following instructions from his father, Earl Collingwood, the Duke of Wellington — or Tom.

Even though the old groom at his aunt's stables had given him directions to the London Road, as he rode along he wished he had the groom with him to help him find the way in the lonely countryside. A blustery wind and mistiness made Charlie aware that daylight was fading fast. He was savouring the damp earthiness and beauty of the colourful autumn leaves when he became aware of a dog following him.

Skippy had obviously got loose and was bounding along by his horse's galloping feet.

He reined his horse in and shouted, 'Go home, you stupid hound!'

Skippy sat panting with his tongue hanging out, and looked up adoringly at the man he now regarded as his master.

'Oh well, I have not the time to return you. Just behave yourself!'

Charlie decided that when he got to the next post house he would pay a boy to take Skippy back to his aunt's house.

However, he had not yet reached a posting house before he saw in the distance ahead of him what might be an ambush — armed men on the road ahead. Highwaymen? Surely not! They harassed travellers on the main roads, not on country lanes.

Instinctively he wheeled his mount around to ride away, but before he knew it, two men were behind him in the narrow, high-hedged road so there was no means of him avoiding them.

Forcibly reminded of his previous encounter with hostile soldiers at Waterloo, Charlie quailed. He had little money with him, but he had his father's signet ring which he must protect.

Pretending to fall off his horse, as if they had frightened him, Charlie landed on the ground with a painful jar to his leg. Whistling softly to Skippy, the yapping, furry animal came to him gladly. Under the pretence of examining his sore leg, he took the signet ring off his tasselled boot and, as he had done before, slipped the ring onto the dog's collar. The animal nuzzled close and remained still, as if understanding what was required.

Charlie soon guessed who the highwaymen were when he heard them speak in French after coming closer.

Their coarse, merciless treatment of him when they hauled him to his feet made it clear they knew who he was; they were Lenoir's brigands who had followed him to England.

How they could possibly have found him was a mystery — until he saw slumped on a horse the ill-treated body of poor Tom.

Lenoir's men must have tortured Tom into revealing where he could be found in England — and the ring.

Not condemning Tom — as Charlie knew he too would have told them where the ring was if they were thus cruel to him — Charlie realised that only his wits would save him and Tom from being dispatched forthwith. Consequently, he pretended he had no idea why they were attacking him. Brave Skippy was snarling, attempting to defend his master.

Tom was unconscious, and Charlie was unable to understand the French they spoke as they threatened and searched him. The brigands grew angry, wondering if Tom had led them to the right person. Charlie was not dressed like an aristocrat and he had nothing valuable on him, nor even much money.

After suffering several blows, Charlie became faint and then unconscious. The brigands began to argue about whether he was in fact Lord Chard because he was not wearing the best quality gentleman's clothes.

Charlie had acted as though he was an ordinary, unsuspecting traveller, who had no idea why he was being attacked. The blows stopped when their torturers realised both Charlie and Tom were unconscious — and had to be left for a while to recover before they could extract any information about the ring they wanted.

They were dragged towards a five-bar gate, which was opened so the brigands could take him and Tom into an empty farm shed and dump them on the muddy floor. It was unnecessarily savage for the Frenchmen to kick Skippy, who yelped pitifully and ran off as they hauled their prisoners into the shed.

Regaining partial consciousness, it only made Charlie angry and more determined to survive this inhumane treatment and eventually exact revenge. His school French bore no resemblance to the patois of these simple louts and Charlie could not understand what they were shouting at him — even if he had wanted to reveal the whereabouts of the signet ring.

One Frenchman shouted, 'Comrades, let's go for a drink and put our feet up until daylight. By then these Englishmen will be recovered enough for us to continue questioning them about where to find the ring.'

The vicious, largely simple brigands, sloped off to look for a nearby inn, leaving their prisoners well tied up, but unguarded.

As soon as Charlie and Tom were left alone, Charlie assessed their situation. Moans came from Tom's gagged mouth as he became semi-conscious. Charlie had a filthy rag stuck in his mouth too, his hands and ankles bound uncomfortably tight.

His only comfort was that the dog had returned after one of the men had kicked him and made him yelp and run away. But even so, Skippy could not untie them, could he?

Charlie sweated in terror, suffering flashbacks to his ordeal after the battle of Waterloo.

★   ★   ★

In the autumn months, daylight came later but the farmer's cattle still needed milking even during the morning darkness. The French brigands had carelessly left the farm gate open. The cows, who were ready for their early morning milking, began straying out of the field and along the lane into the farmyard, waking the farm dogs, and disturbing the ducks by the pond who began quacking in an agitated state.

Dairyman Sam Puddifat was wakened too and did not appreciate having to begin his day even earlier than normal because his herd had somehow managed to open their field gate and had got out.

Looking out of his bedroom window he noticed his farm dogs had been joined by another stray dog. Grabbing his long gun, he determined to shoot the beast that had caused the chaos.

By the time he had dressed, rounded up his cows and driven them towards the milking shed, he realised the new dog was no trouble. In fact the amiable beast was a help in rounding up the wanderers and did not need to be shot after all.

Neither he, nor his cows, expected to find two tightly bound men lying on the milking shed floor!

'Blimey!' Sam exclaimed, examining his find, and noticing the captives' wounded state. Victims of footpads, he reckoned.

The dog was whining, and kept pawing the ground near one of the men, and Sam guessed the dog belonged to him.

In his mind, no dog would try and protect a bad master, so Sam set about releasing Viscount Charles.

Mumbled words and pleas for help made Sam wonder if he was doing the right thing untying the prisoners, especially as he did not want to get involved in anything unsavoury. But when he understood one claimed to be Viscount Chard — and he knew Lady Matilda Chard lived not far away — he thought he had better assist them, as it seemed to him that the two bound men had been victims of highwaymen.

He was the herdsman for the local magistrate, Mr Archibald Smith, and his first job that morning was to hurry to the big house and report his find.

Mr Smith was not unused to dealing with lawbreakers, and although it was still early, he soon sent his lawmen to investigate the strange tale his herdsman had reported, and to find out if one of the men Sam had found was indeed Lord Charles Chard. Although what his lordship was doing on his dairy farm at the crack of dawn, he simply could not imagine. But then rich young men, as Lord Chard was — especially young unmarried men — did tend to get up to all kinds of mischief to amuse themselves!

13

Next day, after breakfast in bed brought by Molly, Amy was requested to join Aunt Matilda.

Molly, looking bright, informed Amy that she had sorted out clean clothes for both of them in the linen room. Molly herself looked smart in her freshly laundered servant's dress and apron.

'Can't say that I like this dress I've found for you, ma'am. It's the sort of dress a governess would wear, but beggars can't be choosers. At least it's clean and will fit you 'til we get your luggage that seems to have got lost.'

Amy was only too glad to have clean linen and a dress that fitted her, and her hair nicely done. By mid-morning she was ready to face Charlie's aunt. She told herself that whatever she looked like, she was now a viscountess. She had status and the security of knowing

Viscount Chard — even if he did not actually love her — regarded her with respect, so she could hold her head up high and withstand any criticism of her dress.

On entering the saloon she found to her surprise another lady present. Lady Jersey, a respected lady of fashion, had come on a morning visit to see her old friend, Matilda. Amy was conscious of the sharp examination she was given by the society lady as she came forward and curtsied.

Aunt Matilda called to her, 'Come and kiss me good morning, Amy. Don't be afraid of Lady Jersey. She might be a stickler in Society, but we ain't in society here!'

Matilda turned to her lady friend and explained, 'My nephew and his new wife turned up on my doorstep yesterday, all dishevelled, as if they had just escaped from a French prison, don't you know! As you can see, we have patched her up with the only ladies' wear I had in the house that would fit her.'

'Oh, do tell me more,' Lady Jersey said eagerly.

This gossip held great interest for her, having been told about the execution of the King and Queen of France, and the mob's cruel treatment of the aristocracy. Afraid the same wave of mob revolution might surge across the Channel, and the English aristocrats might be next in line for the guillotine, she shuddered.

As Amy realised the two ladies wished simply to hear of her experiences aboard, she was happy to sit with them and regale them with tales of how her husband had lost his ring and had to journey to France to reclaim it. She refrained however from telling her tale in a manner that would upset the ladies, nor did she attempt to dramatise what had occurred.

Choosing her words carefully and avoiding describing the worst parts of her honeymoon adventure, Amy was able to entertain them without making herself out to be a heroine.

Lady Jersey was full of admiration on hearing the account of their escape. Lifting her delicate hands in dismay she exclaimed, 'Goodness me! Thank the good Lord you got away safely.'

Aunt Matilda was silently gratified to hear how her nephew had been transformed from a pleasure-loving, although dutiful son, into a warrior fighting his own battles.

A polite rap on the door announced the butler, who brought an urgent message for Lady Matilda from her neighbour, Archibald Smith. He had written to tell her that his herdsmen claimed he had found Viscount Chard tied up in his milking shed early this morning, all battered about! Presumably he was a victim of highwaymen, as was the other man found with him.

So, her nephew had got himself into a pickle! But she would not criticise his misfortune in front of Lady Jersey, and have the story broadcast all over Society. Whatever disaster had befallen Charlie, she felt sure he had enough bravery and intelligence to get over it.

'Well, I never!' was all she said.

Amy's hands flew to her face in alarm and she cried, 'Where is Lord Charles now?'

The butler replied, 'I understand his lordship and another injured man were taken to Mr Smith's manor house as Mr Smith is the local magistrate. The two men were in a poor way — one not short of death — and had to be attended by a doctor. But Lord Chard, although also severely beaten, would not stay to recover from his ordeal. His lordship insisted on being taken to London immediately. So the magistrate sent him to the capital in his carriage with an armed guard.'

The ladies' startled eyes blinked rapidly at this astounding news.

The butler went on, 'Mr Smith wishes you to know that he has called for armed men to arrest these rogue Frenchmen. The villains are apparently French, although Mr Smith does not fully understand Lord Chard's explanation as to why they are over here roaming the countryside and attacking our countrymen. However, Mr Smith wishes everyone to be informed, as he fears they are very dangerous.'

Having delivered this account of the morning's events, the butler took in a deep breath and added, 'Mr Smith has given the order that everyone in the neighbourhood is to be on the alert for a possible attack. Children should be kept in, women should bolt their doors, and men be ready to shoot any Frenchman they find on their property.'

The three ladies in the salon shivered — Amy especially, as she was horrified to learn that Monsieur Lenoir's tentacles had reached even across the Channel.

Aunt Matilda, with admirable composure, rose from her chair and immediately issued orders to protect her house. Outside doors were locked and the window shutters were to be closed — although the daylight was bathing the gardens with a lively glow.

Lady Jersey realised her short morning visit was about to be extended until they had word that all the Frenchmen had been rounded up — although no one knew how many there were on the loose. Her ladyship sensibly saw no point having the vapours, and was pleased to see her hostess and her niece behaved sensibly too.

It was an opportunity for Lady Jersey to get to know the Viscountess Amy Chard, who behaved admirably, she thought. A young woman she would have no hesitation to allow to be introduced to Polite Society, after all the hide-and-seek games of chasing foreign footpads was over.

Fortunately, Aunt Matilda was excited as much as afraid at the news. Her domestic staff, she felt sure, were well able to bar the windows and doors, and the cook was thrilled to be able to provide the kind of meals she liked to prepare instead of the mistress's light snacks. Thus, the whole household was buzzing with activity, every servant enjoying the unusual turn of events.

At midday, Skippy turned up barking hungrily for his dinner. Amy's little maid, Molly was thankful to see him safe, as she'd noticed he was missing the preceding night and concluded he had been out rabbiting.

'Where have you been?' she screeched. The dog's coat was so muddy that she was obliged to get the boot boy to help her find a tub and get the animal in it to wash his shaggy coat.

'Larks!' Molly exclaimed after removing the dog's collar and seeing the signet ring looped over it. 'Blimey! If it ain't that bloody ring again! His lordship must have put it there to bring back to Lady Amy. I'll take it to her right away. You get that dog dried up and then fed, lad.'

Lady Jersey found the situation hilarious when Molly barged into the saloon holding the ring aloft. Forgetting to curtsy to the ladies, she shrilled, 'Look, ma'am, Lord Chard must have hid 'is ring on Skippy's collar again. Put the ring onto your garter for safe keeping.'

Lady Jersey tittered.

While Amy hurriedly made excuses for Molly's sudden intrusion and her forthright manner, both of the ladies were thrilled to see the signet ring safe, and saw no reason to tell the maid off, as they had already heard how Molly had bravely retrieved the ring in France.

'Thank you, Molly,' said Aunt Matilda, giving the maid a wink. 'Lady Jersey, Lady Amy and myself will endeavour to hide my brother's ring, which is causing so much trouble. Now, I would suggest that you ask my housekeeper to find you some dry clothes because the dog would appear to have washed you, too.'

When Molly left the saloon with a wide smile, knowing her efforts were appreciated, Lady Jersey announced that she had not been in the slightest bit insulted, and enjoyed her lunch and chat with Amy and her hostess.

Fortunately, Amy's polite and unaffected behaviour was enough to impress the visitor, who assured her of her acceptance in polite society.

Aunt Matilda encouraged Amy to sit with them after lunch when the tea tray was brought in. Lady Jersey was soon engaged in the task of advising Amy on which shops she must visit in Tunbridge Wells, and the sewing maids who would provide her with the up-to-the-minute fashionable clothing she would need in order to be acceptable to members of the ton.

Amy had not expected to be thrust into the midst of the best society, but she now accepted that suddenly her life was to be a round of balls, assemblies, card parties, concerts and theatres. Aunt Matilda would attend very few of them — the old lady preferred to stay quietly at home — but she relished preparing Amy for her role.

Therefore, there was a great deal to discuss, which passed the time pleasantly as the three ladies waited for the emergency to be over.

Amy showed no annoyance at the way in which the two older ladies planned her coming out into Society, almost as though she were a doll they were planning to dress. She smiled politely and warmly at all their suggestions, giving Lady Jersey the impression that Lord Chard's new wife was a charming young woman — and that opinion would soon be circulated around the ton.

Amy's much more pressing concern was for her injured husband. She longed to be with him, to take care of him, although she knew he would have good medical treatment. She was not surprised to learn that Lord Chard was anxious to go to see his bank manager in town, determined to obey his father and settle the financial problems the theft had caused him. On receiving the message that the ring was once more safe at his aunt's house, he had made the briefest of calls — not even stepping inside the door — to collect the signet ring from her hands as he set off back in the magistrate's coach to London, every inch a man on a mission despite the bruises visible on his face and the agonies he must have been feeling.

Amy felt proud of him, but prayed he was safe. She recalled how he had kissed her tenderly as he left her once more, saying, 'I do not know how long I shall be away, Amy. I believe my Aunt Matilda is happy to have you stay here awhile, and I hope you will be happy too.'

Amy had not liked to say that she feared she would feel out-of-place and long to be in her own home, or that she would feel lonely without him.

Now, however, she was glad she had put on a brave face and sent Charlie off with her blessing. Indeed, as things had worked out, she had been accepted by one of society's grandest matrons without having to make any effort at all!

★   ★   ★

After the half dozen French brigands were captured and the magistrate dispatched them to jail, the welcome news was passed around to everyone in the district. Uneventful daily life resumed, although the experience of having foreign devils flying about the countryside was a topic for the village folk to discuss for years to come.

Amy and Matilda settled into a routine. Despite her worry, Amy's stay was largely enjoyable as she was well looked after. She spent days shopping and being measured for new clothes in Tunbridge Wells. She could have succumbed to ennui and melancholy at times, were it not for meals she shared with Aunt Matilda, whom she found to be not only a kind hostess, but frequently very amusing company.

'My dear,' Matilda observed keenly, 'correct me if I am wrong, but I do believe we are wasting our time making you up fashionable new dresses as you will soon be unable to wear them.'

Amy blushed and lowered her eyes.

'You have guessed it, then?'

'I have noted it with delight, my dear. It is a shame we have as yet no news of Charlie so that he can be told of your condition.'

Ruefully Amy agreed. She would love to be the one to tell him that she was with child.

Matilda did not allow Charlie's absence to dim her enthusiasm for preparing Amy for motherhood. Having no children of her own, she did not bombard Amy with advice, but both ladies set about preparing for the baby with great energy.

Amy sent a letter to her mama, and another to Harriet, but was careful not to write anything she felt might upset them. Nothing about her harrowing honeymoon, nor anything boastful about her acceptance in society. Nor indeed that she had lost track of where her husband was — and that he had now been away for some time.

Soon the time would come when her situation was known to them, and her new home ready to receive them, but at present she only wished them to know that she was well and happy, and hoped they would reply and say the same.

She understood why Charlie had to dash up to London, and thence to see his father. Indeed she hardly had time to miss him as she was learning from Aunt Matilda how to run a big household full of servants — as she would soon be required to do when she and Charlie began to live in their own country and town homes.

Although now visibly with child, Amy was able to continue meeting fashionable ladies at home on visits, and she soon acquired some ease in polite company, taking part in their gossip. Not looking for a husband, nor being a young bride, put her in a good position to be welcomed by many she met as a friend rather than a potential rival. She was a newcomer to their fashionable ways and her willingness to be agreeable and to admit her provincial upbringing amused them as much as they were intrigued by meeting the new Viscountess Chard, whom they found to be a woman of great kindness and sense.

Molly seemed well occupied learning how to be a proper maid, although her forthright character would not make her a suitable companion for any fastidious lady — especially when Molly, as well as her mistress, was found to be with child!

Amy wanted to find out where Tom was being cared for, so that she could arrange for him to be reunited with his love — although Molly assured her that her family would look after her, and her child, should Tom not survive his ill-treatment.

★　★　★

What on earth was Charlie up to? Amy wondered.

He had sent a short note to assure her she was not forgotten. He said he had returned the ring to his papa, but that his father also expected his son to sort out the financial mess, and the legalities with the French traders about the misuse of his signet ring would take some while.

Charlie confided to her that he was dismayed to have been asked to take on this protracted and arduous task, but felt it was his duty, therefore he would remain in London until the affair was completely wound up.

As it turned out, the unpleasant business took months. However, there was much for Amy to do, including daily walks with the dog — for the sake of her health as her pregnancy advanced. She had not wanted to tell him about their expected child by post — it did not seem right — but her growing size meant that Aunt Matilda was able to fuss to her heart's content!

'Just as we have your wardrobe in order, now we shall have to add to it!' she announced.

Amy chuckled, knowing Matilda was not at all cross. Having Amy to stay had been invigorating for her — and her staff — and even though she would be glad when the time came for her to return to the quiet life she had enjoyed before Amy had arrived, the old lady had to confess she was enjoying every challenge her visitor brought.

Shopping for an expectant mother and a baby was most diverting for both ladies.

Amy was able to enjoy seeing Tunbridge Wells, with its distinctive Regency buildings including the marvellous Calverley Park Crescent designed by Decimus Burton. It was a wonder for her to behold. The spa itself, like Bath, was a feature of the town; people flocked there seeking a 'cure', the tradesmen flourished and its shops were full of ladies' requirements and luxury items such as perfumes. So there was plenty to interest Amy when she ventured out.

Sometimes she did so with Molly, but avoiding the strutting hours when the rich and famous went out and about, wanting to be seen and admired in their fashionable clothes.

By this time Amy's girth was

increasing rapidly and she was thankful for Aunt Matilda's company now that she was unable to be seen in society.

Aunt Matilda showed great tolerance on hearing that Molly was to have a child too — although she did remark that she wondered what on earth Amy and Molly had been up to in France!

Amy did not care to enlighten anyone on the harrowing aspects of her honeymoon and brushed aside the reason why they had turned up in England looking little better than beggars. Aunt Matilda knew Lord Chard was well provided for, so she shrugged and put aside her questions and misgivings. What people did on their honeymoon was their own affair.

Amy was delighted to receive news of her mother and sister. Two letters arrived, one for Lady Matilda and one for Lady Amy.

'And about time your mama wrote to you,' commented Aunt Matilda, opening her letter from her brother, Earl Chard.

'I suppose she knew not where I was,' replied Amy, avidly reading her correspondence. 'Indeed, Mama explains here in her letter that she has only just heard of Charlie's indisposition.'

'But my nephew is not ill!'

'No, not ill, but I believe he was was badly injured by those French brigands and although he bravely insisted on continuing his journey to his bank in London, he must have been half dead by the time he arrived there. He has been recovering ever since, tending to his business when he is able.'

Aunt Matilda nodded. 'Of course. My brother told me he had been contacted by the bank and that the IOU payments had stopped — which means Charlie achieved his goal, and has to be congratulated for his bravery and determination.'

Amy's face showed her relief. How proud she was of him! But it had been so long now and she was missing him, and fretting over how he fared.

'Before long you will be off to your

new home,' Aunt Matilda observed. 'I shall miss you, my dear.'

Amy walked over and gently kissed the lady who had been a better mother to her than even her own. She said, 'You have been so very kind to me, dearest Aunt Matilda.'

'No more than you deserve. You are ready to begin your proper wedded life, Amy, my dear, and it has been nought but a pleasure for me to be able to help set you up.'

Indeed, Amy was looking forward to it.

Nevertheless, she worried what state Charlie would be in after his ordeal. Was he now an invalid? Why had his father not informed her of his condition — or, indeed, shown appreciation for his signet ring being returned and his finances set in order? All Charlie's father had done was to write to his sister, not to her. And his wife, the Countess Chard, seemed no better than her mama in ignoring her.

Amy's future happiness, and that of

her child, depended upon her husband — and the longer he stayed away the more she began to doubt . . .

How would she manage on her own, in her husband's large establishments, without Aunt Matilda to support her? Misgivings of all kinds assailed her.

However, her unborn child must be her main concern for now. She was much occupied in taking advice from all who were anxious to give it — and there were many old wives' tales she had to fend off.

Molly too was becoming too heavy to work with as much vigour as she used to. In her cheery way she was not upset when her role was changed to that of a maid of all light work, and Amy took on a new lady's maid.

Amy had made enquiries about Tom, and discovered he had been recovering in a London military hospital. Molly's family were informed too, and soon, much to Amy's delight, plans were being made for Tom and Molly to marry and a home being prepared for them.

All too soon, it was time for Molly to leave for her new home and married life. Amy embraced her feisty companion and bade her a fond farewell. After she left, she missed her humour and bubbly chatter greatly.

Being idle did not suit Amy, now that her heavily pregnant condition obliged her to keep apart from society's activities. She had no work to do in Aunt Matilda's house so she tried to keep herself busy by entertaining the old lady, sewing baby clothes, and daily walks with her dog. Reading and being driven around in a small carriage made pleasant diversions too.

Her confinement would not last forever, Amy kept reminding herself. Soon she would be fully engaged in childcare. So she was determined to make the best of all the leisure time she had before she was launched into motherhood.

14

Rain was lashing across the window as the morning light seemed reluctant to brighten up the day, but after all, it was wintertime.

Bored with the stitchery she was doing, Amy straightened her aching back. Her baby was becoming too heavy for her to sit comfortably for long. In the parlour it was necessary for a candle to be lit so she could see what she was doing, and so she put her sewing things away.

It should be lunchtime soon. Having no duties, as Aunt Matilda's staff were capable of running the household, Amy looked forward to having her own house to run. But being a guest in Matilda's house, she had to be careful not to interfere with the way the servants did their work. From the stiff butler Martin, to the lowest kitchen maid, they all treated her respectfully, as she also tried to be pleasant to them.

Suddenly, from outside the window, she heard Skippy barking wildly. What was he making such a noise about?

Amy went to find out.

A curricle had arrived at the front door and, moving the window curtain aside to get a better look, she saw the tall, lithe figure of a gentleman stepping out of the carriage and handing his hat and cloak to the butler as he entered the hall, while Skippy yelped joyously and danced around his boots.

'Quiet!' the man commanded and instantly the dog was.

Amy blinked as she recognised his voice and she hurried to the parlour door.

'Her ladyship is currently in the saloon,' the butler informed the well-attired gentleman. 'Your aunt likes a nap after she has had her lunch.'

'I wish to see my wife first, Martin.'

Amy gasped. Her husband had returned at last!

Shyness attacked her, made her feel

glued to the door frame which she held onto for support. For so long she had longed for this moment, but now it had come she was shocked, unable to rush and greet him.

'Amy! Amy!'

She heard his commanding voice calling her, yet still she could not bring herself to move forward to greet him.

In the months they had been apart, the close intimacy of their one night together had faded almost from memory.

Amy was shaking — what was she to do? She knew she must move to greet him, and she so longed to do so, yet her feet would not budge. However, she did not have to move because all of a sudden he was there beside her.

After all the waiting for him, the longing to see him again, Amy felt as if she was facing a stranger. Attired in best quality jacket and freshly scented linen, buckskin pantaloons tucked into shiny boots, he presented himself as an aristocrat should in his perfect morning dress.

Firm hands clasped her shoulders as

he drew her close.

'Amy, whatever is the matter? Why the tears? I thought you would be glad to see me.'

'Oh, Charlie, of course I am! But I hardly recognise the way you are now.'

'Nor I you, for that matter, for you are twice the size you were, my darling!'

She smiled through her tears. 'I carry your child,' she explained unnecessarily.

'Indeed, I had heard — and I am delighted.'

Taking one of her hands he lifted it and pressed it to his lips, which drew her attention to his face. There she observed a battle-scarred appearance that shocked her. Gone were any boyish looks he used to have. Although still handsome, now with the hardened looks of a warrior, he had become a formidable man.

Swallowing she said, 'I can see how you must have suffered . . . tell me . . .'

'Indeed I shall. But it is a long story, and I think you should sit down first.'

Showing his care for her — or was it for the coming baby? — made her realise that whatever hardships he had suffered since she last saw him it had not taken away his gentle manners and thoughtfulness for others.

A discreet cough behind them made them turn to see Martin standing there.

'My lord, your aunt wishes to see you.'

Charlie laughed. 'I wager she does! This is the second time I have burst into her house unbidden and unexpected and, despite her good nature, I do not wish to displease her. Take my arm, Amy, and we shall go to her straight away. Tell her ladyship we will be with her presently, but that neither of us can run, Martin.'

Viscount Charles Chard, her husband, had become slightly domineering, she noticed — more like his father, Earl Chard. Even with his limp, he strutted a little as though he was in charge of himself, and could cope with any situation. As if he had become used to giving orders and having them obeyed.

A slightly different man had returned to her.

Then again, she too was changed from the country girl she used to be. Now she was not only pregnant, but well dressed, and had acquired the polish necessary for her to mix with the top people in society. She realised that just as he would have to accept he had lost the inexperienced young woman he had married, so she would have to accept the changes he had undergone.

She hoped, as he escorted her towards the saloon and his waiting aunt, that their acquired maturity would bring them happiness together.

She already knew that he would treat her well, but could she hope that he might now love her?

★   ★   ★

'Well, well, nephew Charlie. At least you are presentable today!' chuckled Aunt Matilda, as she adjusted her cap that had fallen askew during her morning nap.

Lord Charles bowed.

267

'Good morning, ma'am,' he said formally. 'I am glad to see you well. I thank you for taking such good care of my wife these past few months.'

'Oh, don't stand there, both of you. Sit down.'

Charlie escorted Amy to a chair and then sat on another so that the three of them were close enough to chat.

'I should like to know what you've been up to — vanishing from Polite Society as you did.'

Charlie replied, 'I know I have a great deal to explain about my absence, but I assure you, I am come as soon as I could — and am in need of refreshment before I tell my tale, for I had no breakfast this morning.'

'Really? Well, we cannot let him starve, can we, Amy? Although I don't know that he deserves anything more from me.'

Amy knew the old lady was joking, as she looked at Charlie fondly — but it was not her house to order the cook to make a meal for him.

Charlie smiled as he sat back in his chair. He crossed his legs and rubbed his hands together in an elegant fashion that showed him to be a gentleman used to dealing with any disagreeable situation.

'As it is almost one,' he said, not in the least put out, 'I warrant that you will get very hungry indeed waiting for luncheon until I tell all that has happened to me!'

Aunt Matilda chuckled.

'Considering your condition, Amy, I venture we should not delay our meal.' She picked up a small silver bell by her chair and rang it. 'Do you require any particular dish, my lord?'

Martin must have been waiting nearby as he came into the room quickly. On being told to ask the cook to provide an extra meal, he said, 'The kitchen staff are already seeing to it, ma'am.'

'Goodness me! This house runs itself!'

'Your kindness runs it, ma'am,' said Charlie.

'Yes,' agreed Amy. 'I have stayed here

long enough to know the affectionate regard in which she is held by her staff and how they anticipate your aunt's needs.'

She wanted to add that she hoped she would be able to run such a happy household — although having children around would give their own servants a great deal of extra work!

★　★　★

Behaving like a perfect guest during the meal, and keeping the conversation light-hearted with no mention of what he was to tell them later, Charlie demonstrated his newly-acquired manner of a titled man capable of taking on the role of an Earl with its many responsibilities. He did mention that his town house and country house had been undergoing modernisation, ready for his new family to live in.

Amy wondered if she would have any say in the matter — they were to be her homes, too.

Charlie regaled them with details of the structural repair work and alterations such as bathrooms being added, describing the latest modern water closets they were to have.

Amy could only imagine how delightful it would be for her and her family, especially when Charlie announced that the choice of furnishings was to be made by her. She was warmed to think that he had been thinking of her during his absence and that her comfort and pleasure were his concern.

'I saw Horatio when I was recovering in hospital, and he told me about all the latest inventions,' explained Charlie. He dabbed his mouth with his serviette as though he was finally beginning to feel full after a huge meal of roast beef, sizzled potatoes, vegetables from the kitchen garden, and horseradish sauce.

'And did you see my sister, Harriet?'

'Indeed I did, Amy.'

'Is she well?'

'She is very well — very much as you are.'

Amy beamed, knowing he meant that her sister was also with child! Suddenly Amy did not feel so much alone. She was so grateful that her husband had been in touch with her family and that his friendship with Horatio — and his wife — was still intact.

They went on to discuss Amy's family and Charlie informed the ladies that he had been on a quick visit to see Amy's mama, and that he found Lady Gibbon in good health despite her many complaints. That made Amy laugh as she knew how dramatic her mama could be in describing her afflictions. By now the diners had reached the dessert course and a hearty apple pie with custard seemed to disappear rapidly as Charlie approached having his fill.

He went on to tell Amy that her mama had been given a smart new carriage and horses, and funds — together with an enthusiastic estate manager to bring her abode up to scratch.

Becoming alarmed at the cost of all this building work and munificent gifts,

Amy ceased to be pleased when he further announced he had bought a new carriage and horses for his Aunt Matilda to go shopping in Tunbridge Wells. Having noticed how impoverished her stables were he felt it was his duty to repay her for all she had done for Amy.

'That lot must have cost you a pretty penny!' Aunt Matilda remarked.

Charlie did not deny it.

'We are not going to retire and leave you with a bottle of port,' declared Matilda. 'You shall only go to sleep after all you have eaten, and we want to hear all about your life after you left here and were caught by those French ruffians.'

'Ah, yes,' agreed Charlie, chuckling. 'So now I must sing for my supper.'

'Quite right!' his hostess returned smartly. 'Now you must entertain us. I shall have the coffee brought into the saloon.'

'What if *you* fall asleep while I tell my tale?'

Aunt Matilda's eyes twinkled. 'Then you shall have to continue after I wake — take Amy and that brute of a dog of yours out in the grounds for a walk. The rain has stopped, although it is muddy underfoot, with a chilly wind out there too. But exercise in the fresh air, if you wrap up well, is beneficial for your unborn child.'

Charlie laughed. It was so good for Amy to hear him in such good spirits, as she was sure he had been through hell since they had parted back in the autumn. And she was about to hear all about that hell as she sipped her coffee . . .

⋆　⋆　⋆

Lord Charles Chard began by informing the ladies that as he had left them to hurry to London to his bank many weeks ago, he had no idea what was in store for him. His main concern, as he was sure they remembered, was to see the bank manager about the fraudulent use of his father's signet ring. To stop any more payments being made to creditors of Monsieur Lenoir, the former secretary to a French Marquis who had been guillotined, who was now leading a band of vicious brigands in northern France.

Charlie took a deep breath, preparing to embark on recalling all that had happened to him.

'As you know, my journey to London was interrupted soon after I left this house. Some of Lenoir's brutes had journeyed to England after capturing Tom, who had told them — after being tortured — where to find me and the signet ring. I am aware you probably have heard all about that part of the story.'

'We did, of course,' Aunt Matilda said promptly. 'Mr Smith, our magistrate, was very quick to let the county know that an army of French villains were loose, and instructed us all to lie low and bolt the doors — which we did, expecting to have to defend ourselves.

However, our only visitor was Skippy, that dog of yours, who turned up with the jewelled signet ring threaded through his collar. Lady Jersey was visiting and thoroughly enjoyed the drama!'

'She would,' Charlie declared. 'Society ladies spend their days gossiping.'

'That may be so, Charlie, but they do not go out and shoot to kill one another as men do!'

Charlie laughed. 'Not all women are as pleasant as you, my dear Aunt Matilda.'

Matilda raised her hand to brush off the compliment and instructed him to continue with his story.

'I will, but I shall get through it much faster if you do not keep interrupting me,' he said with a grin. 'After I was caught, and almost slaughtered by those French bullies,' he stroked a scar on his face, 'I felt almost ready to die, but — '

'Mr Smith told us you were in a bad way but you insisted on continuing on your journey to London, and as we know, he lent you his smart carriage and coachman, and an escort of armed men. Once you received my message that the ring had been brought back here by the dog, you called here to collect it and then off you went again.' Aunt Matilda was not going to be silenced by her nephew in her own home!

Charlie's grey eyes turned to look at Amy.

'I want you to understand that I needed to prove myself. Although I had been with the Duke of Wellington's army, Tom had looked after me, instructed me — just as my father had done — and was keen to protect me. Now, I was on my own with a task only I could do, to get to the bank and notify the Bow Street Runners to round up the Frenchmen. I felt like giving up and sinking into my pain, but I knew that, however injured I was, I must carry on. And so I did. Even if I did land up in hospital in London after my ordeal was over.'

Amy looked with awed, pitying eyes

at her husband. How he must have suffered!

'What a terrible experience for you!'

She thought with anguish about how she had spent time enjoying shopping and socialising in Tunbridge Wells while he was hospitalised.

'It was my choice, Amy. I could have refused to join the army and still be enjoying life as a man about town like many gentlemen of my age. Instead I intended to complete the tasks my father set me. Now, having accomplished them, I am waiting to become a father myself . . . '

Amy's face flushed.

'It will not be long,' she said barely audibly as she felt the infant's movement inside her.

'So, what exactly have you been doing to feel so proud of yourself?' his aunt asked briskly.

Charlie's serious face relaxed into a grin.

'As soon as I was recovered enough to leave hospital I made contact with

Tom, whose injuries were far greater than mine. I felt responsible for his disabling injuries — after all, he had sustained them while working for me. Consequently, I arranged for young Molly, who was by then at her parents' home, to go and look after him. I discovered they intended to marry anyway so it was not difficult to assist in setting them up in a comfortable home of their own.'

'Well, that was a commendable thing to have done, Charlie, but it is your own home and coming family that you should have been thinking about!' Matilda wagged her finger at him.

'My dear aunt, I knew that you were looking after Amy admirably. No, I had another job to do.'

'What on earth could you possibly have to keep you away for so long?'

'Justice had to be my next urgent concern,' Charlie explained. 'That French villain had got away with bringing a great deal of suffering to many people. Amy will recall one poor family she saw in France, whose livelihood had been destroyed by his brigands. They had been cruel to so many.'

'Yes, I do remember that family,' Amy nodded. 'The farmer had been turned off his land, his animals taken, his wife expecting another child — and the children she had were starving.'

She shuddered, thinking how awful it would be had she not been cared for at this time.

Charlie continued, 'It was clear to me that something should be done to end Monsieur Lenoir's reign of terror. As it had been funded by my father's ring, and because I had suffered personally at the hands of that band of brigands, I saw it as my duty. So, I went back to France and told the authorities in Paris they should put a stop to Monsieur Lenoir's evil.'

'How brave! Especially as France seem set against aristocrats!' Amy cried, full of admiration for her husband.

'No, Amy — the French are over their reign of terror and have reinstated their royalty and aristocrats. Now they are reorganising themselves, replacing the old order with new laws and an administration Napoleon has set out for them — although he is not in charge any longer. It is a national social upheaval that has changed for the better, although it will take time and be difficult for some to adjust to. But, of course, I could not wait around to see what they will do about criminals like Monsieur Lenoir.'

Amy could imagine his gloom as he recalled it.

Suddenly Charlie sat up straight, and said, as if recalling a dream, 'I felt I was not obeying my father, nor a senior army officer, but was merely doing the right thing when I returned to Lille and tried to assemble a small army of volunteers to rout out the troublemakers. It was not easy, as many were afraid of the brigands. And I was used to obeying orders, not giving them. Their way of talking often foxed me too. They were familiar with the district, though — and we formed a plan.'

Suddenly Aunt Matilda gave a gentle snore and her head had rolled to one side. Amy got up to adjust the cushions so that she could take her after-dinner nap in comfort.

'Just as well she's fallen asleep at that juncture,' remarked Charlie. 'Some of what happened in our attack on the chateau was not pleasant . . . '

'Then I do not wish to hear it either,' Amy said firmly, returning to her seat and moving her chair nearer to Charlie so that they could chat together quietly.

He put out his hand to take one of hers. It was comforting, and Amy smiled at him.

'I confess to feeling skittish these days,' she explained. 'After all, I am about to give birth and all the dangers that might entail . . . well, shall we say it is not something I look forward to.'

'All will be well, my love,' Charlie said softly and leaned forward to kiss her cheek. 'And I shall not regale you with the gory details of our assault — only how we achieved the triumph!'

15

Amy was eager to hear how her husband had successfully destroyed the bandit-controlled chateau, but she was even more elated that he had shown her a genuine sign of affection.

His normal good manners she appreciated, but hearing him call her 'my love' sounded as though he really meant it!

Dismissing her wish for him to say or do anything further to reinforce the emotion behind his endearment was easier because he plunged immediately into describing his feat . . .

'The difficulty we faced was that there was no official backing for what I was intending to do. As I found out, just as in Paris, the local officials were not planning to round up the brutal band of brigands yet. They told us they had other urgent government matters to attend to. I had no wish to hang around Lille for months, so I realised that I had to organise the raiding party to destroy the power of the criminals myself.'

Charlie rubbed his hand over his face and eyes as if remembering the dilemma he had been in.

'I am not naturally aggressive, and without Tom by my side I was at a loss to know even how to start. If I put up a notice to try and recruit volunteers in the neighbourhood, the brigands would see it and be on their guard. So I had to approach people quietly to find enough men to storm the chateau without alerting the enemy.

'Also, we had no weapons to speak of — guns or other means to fight with . . . I experienced a strong desire to return home, to let the French deal with their own problem, but then I pictured Tom again and how badly the brigands had treated him. He had helped me retrieve the signet ring and so had little Molly. I simply had to think of a way — and quickly, as I longed to get back to you, my love.'

There — he had said it again!

Amy looked at him sharply, but he seemed unware that he had used the words of endearment.

'The winter nights were very cold,' he went on. 'Snow patches lingered here and there with mud everywhere. I tramped around the chateau at night when all the brigands were assembled and raged at their riotous behaviour, drinking wine they had stolen and gorging on food the poor families were desperate for.

'The local people had not the strength without the militia and their weapons to help them. I had my pistol — but what use was one firearm against our well-armed enemies?'

Charlie suddenly slapped his knee. 'Then an idea came to me! As I had been taking care not to be caught in a wolf trap as I walked in the woods, I thought we could set up some similar such traps for the villains. Man traps to catch poachers could be made at the smithy.

'The smiths worked willingly, and secretly,

to make enough traps. The old chateau groundsman set them up one evening. They were placed around the chateau to catch the brigands after we had set fire to the chateau — although I was loath to destroy such a fine building.

'Fearfully, lest we were caught, we blocked most of the chateau windows and doors that night, except where we would place the traps outside so that when the brigands came out, they would be trapped by them.'

'But would they not avoid stepping on the traps when they saw them?' Amy asked.

'Ah, but it was night. We set fires at the doors and they were forced to come out in a panic to get away from the burning building, and could not see the traps in the darkness — until they stepped on one.'

Amy shivered. 'A cruel method to catch them!'

'Indeed — but war is cruel.'

There was silence in the room for a moment.

Then Amy said, 'What happened then?'

A shrill voice piped up as Aunt Matilda awoke from her nap. 'We have no wish to hear every single gory detail, Amy!'

Amy agreed. She could always ask Charlie to tell her more about the operation later. This was a time to rejoice. Smiling, she clapped her hands, saying, 'Well done!'

Charlie's lips lifted into a smile.

'You are quite right, Aunt Matilda. The action we took was a gamble. It could have been me, or my men, who perished. However, owing to the local people's determination to banish the brigands, and them not dreaming that they would ever be attacked, it worked well enough.'

'And Monsieur Lenoir?'

'He was caught with the rest. For me, and for those he had harmed, it was a well-deserved end to his villainy.'

'Did he die?' Amy gasped.

'I know not. I saw some of the brigands being overpowered, some shot, and others released from the man traps. Afterwards the injured were carted off to prison and we were satisfied the nest of hornets was destroyed — with their leader.

'The necessity for me staying away from you for so long was over, and I returned on the first available passenger ferry.

'Now I want only to forget about my adventures and misfortune in France, and concentrate on my family here in England.'

At last Charlie felt he had earned his place in the world, and was worthy of wearing his ancestor's signet ring, and looking forward expectantly for his wife to give him a son and heir.

Aunt Matilda nodded.

'Quite right, too! You have a great deal to do now. Your child is due very soon, and while my sewing maids have been busy making clothes, the poor child as yet has nowhere to lay its head.'

Laughing, Charlie said, 'Then we shall set off for our own home tomorrow. I am sure you will not want a squalling baby in your house, aunt.'

'No, I would not! A tea party with elegant ladies and gossip is as much disturbance as I need these days.' But she smiled as she added, 'Naturally I shall miss you, and will look forward to your news and your next visit.'

Charlie went to his aunt, kneeling awkwardly beside her.

'How can I thank you for your kindness to us?'

'Oh, hush, you need not. I confess it has been fun. That is not to say I shan't slip back into my retired life quite easily, nonetheless. And I shall *not* miss your dog, which my staff tell me has not been the quietest or cleanest of guests . . . although they love him,' she added with a wink.

* * *

Amy was anxious to see their new country home. Well, new to her, for it was not a new house, parts of it being very old indeed. It had been a medieval castle originally, with additions build on over the centuries. The oldest part of the property had been left to crumble with only the grass around it mowed. The newer part was still old and had required the services of an architect to redesign its interior for comfortable living.

Charlie had previously ignored his country house, his youth being spent far away from it, although he had made sure the property had been looked after in his absence. So it was not in too dreadful a state, and the architect turned out to be a lucky choice in that he had taken great pride in the rebuilding as well as modernising the living area.

Amy loved the countryside around the house, and she was fascinated by the castle ruins, as well as excited about the new, modern fittings.

'Oh, I do love it, Charlie!' she breathed as she explored with her husband.

Needless to say, Skippy also approved of his new home.

Charlie was delighted to know that Amy approved of what he had done.

'The building work is done, so now it is up to you to decorate our rooms,' he told her.

A few months ago, she would have been daunted at the prospect of shopping for the furnishings, but not now; having been schooled by Aunt Matilda and educated by her new circle of friends, she felt equal to the challenge. In fact she was quite glad she did not have the tastes of her mama, or young sister, to take into account. Her decisions, and choices were for Charlie and herself — and the new child.

She was pleased, too, that her in-laws lived far enough way not to overly bother her. Charlie had mentioned that his mother had made the assumption that they would be living with her — and had been busy with preparing a nursery at her house.

'Oh dear! I hope your mama is not upset to learn we do not intend to move in.'

Charlie shrugged. 'My old nursery will be useful when we visit them with our children,' he said.

Our children! Amy had not even thought beyond the arrival of their first child.

She had had no time to consider more than the immediate future; making sure their private rooms were comfortable and pleasing for them both, hiring staff and deciding on which local shops would provide them with provisions.

Their neighbours, too, had to be known, and Amy was grateful to Aunt Matilda for the training she had been given in how to cope with older visitors.

★ ★ ★

Viscount Charles Chard knew that for all his achievements, he had lost some things too, since he had attempted to better himself.

He had gained self-esteem, experience to run his affairs and the respect of his employees. He had lost some of his youthful physical charm, now having a few scars on his body and even his face.

And his leg, injured at Waterloo, was a permanent, if slight, disability.

He underestimated his mature good looks, which made women turn to admire the tall aristocrat, but he been brought up to be a gentleman, and so he was. He had never been coarse or rude in his manner — although he could cut people effectually when he wished to!

He did not notice the warmth in Amy's eyes when she saw him approach, nor observe the pride she felt when talking about him to others.

He would overhear her say, 'I think my husband would like this,' as though he was not present and she could not ask him what he wanted.

She never spoke to him of her worries or desires. She behaved as though she was supposed to keep her feelings to herself. She had been brought up to be a lady — not a lady of fashion perhaps, but nevertheless a gentlewoman — with certain standards of conduct and behaviour, so it was natural for her to continue in that way.

She had also had a mother and sister who never put her first, so she did not expect to be more than a useful person, enjoying what she could in her life — but not expecting her husband to provide her with constant pleasures.

'What can I buy you in town, Amy?' Charlie would ask her, hoping she would tell him what perfume she would like, or some other feminine pleasure. Yet she never did ask him for anything and it hurt him that she was unable to be open with him.

Unbeknown to him, all Amy longed for was for him to declare his love for her!

Perhaps he *did* love her — he certainly behaved as if he did — but she longed to hear him say so.

'Oh, you have spent enough recently,' she would smile up at him. 'Our baby is not royalty to require the best of everything.'

'I was thinking of you, not the baby.'

'Charlie. I have been spoiled with so many things. Why not spend your money on one of those newly invented engines?'

There! She had once again turned to something he would like — and she was clever to have spotted his keen interest in inventions like the latest steam engines.

So many opportunities were opening up with the invention of the railways, even farm machines instead of using the usual method of employing men with scythes.

'I am pleased to see you take an interest in modern machinery,' she added. 'After all, I benefit too — I do so love to take a bath in our new bathroom, Charlie.'

Thus Lord Charles was reassured that his wife was happy and he should be too. Yet he still felt she was not totally in harmony with him. Something in their relationship was missing. She had not told him she loved him since the early days of their whirlwind courtship, and it irked him that she seemed to avoid any opportunities for close communication between them, brushing away on some excuse to be busy with some work she had to get on with.

Naturally Amy was content with all her material goods — only she sometimes felt that someone else could well be in her shoes. He was merely being kind and thoughtful, perhaps because he had a guilty conscience in the hasty manner he had married her only to suit his father's command to produce an heir.

Amy thought it because he did not love her.

No, the truth was that Charles and Amy were still unable to tell each other of their feelings for each other. It had become a habit with them to keep emotionally apart — neither confessing their need to admit they were indeed in love.

Charlie did not see that the situation was in any way his fault, or that he held the key to her total happiness. He had come to understand army life, but married life was still a mystery to him — like his wife's smile at times.

Something he feared he had not quite grasped the meaning of. He loved her, but was not sure she loved him.

His greatest achievement was that he had acquired a more than suitable wife. Amy, to his deep satisfaction, had turned out to be a perfect partner for him. At least, he thought so. But the success of his hurried marriage of convenience, was not he feared, shared by her.

In fact, Amy sometimes felt as lonely as if she had not even married at all, and all her delightful surroundings merely good fortune.

However, she was also aware, day by day that something wonderful was about to happen — and she hoped fervently that the birth of her child would bring her the love she yearned for.

16

On an unusually cold summer morning an old-fashioned nobleman's carriage bowled up the drive towards Viscount Chard's country house.

The coachman was thankful they had arrived, as the gatekeeper's tardiness had added to the ill-temper of the gentleman inside the draughty, ill-sprung coach. It had been a long journey for the old Earl Collingwood. He would normally not have set foot outside his own house unless he considered it important to do so.

Once outside the front portico he was helped out of the coach and into the hall as he continued complaining.

'My wife sent me,' he muttered.

Indeed, his wife had said it was about time. But then she had not had to make the uncomfortable journey — although she had said it was his own fault for not buying a new, better sprung carriage.

'It is not as if you cannot afford one,' she had scolded him.

Earl Collingwood had replied. 'What's the use in having an expensive carriage made? We never go anywhere.'

Now he realised his error and determined that he would take his son's carriage back home after the visit, as Charles employed one of the finest carriage makers and his equipage would be smooth-riding and well cushioned — and certainly not draughty, like his own! The Earl was proud of his son, even if he did not always show it.

As the coach halted outside the front door, the double doors opened to reveal a well liveried servant, ready to greet him.

'Good day, my lord.' Lord Chard's butler recognised the viscount's father, and bowed politely, then quickly came forward to assist the earl into the house.

'Damn it — it's as cold in here as it was outside in the coach!' the earl complained, peeling off his scarf and gloves, which he threw at the butler who caught them deftly.

He used his silver-topped came to stomp towards one of the downstairs rooms.

'Isn't there a fire anywhere in this house?'

His loud voice boomed through the great house and sent the servants running to make one up.

'We have the latest heating system, but not in summer as we do not need it, my lord,' explained the bobbing house-keeper, recognising her master's father.

'Oh, don't we? Well, your new-fangled system is not much use, is it? My hands are frozen! I like to see a blaze in a well-filled grate.'

The Earl of Collingwood had arrived unexpectedly at his son's country house to inspect his grandchild.

'So where is the infant I was told was born a few weeks ago?' he demanded.

The unflappable butler enquired calmly, 'Which infant did you wish to see, my lord?'

The earl looked at the man with raised brows.

'My grandchild — my son's heir, of course!'

'Father!'

Viscount Charles Chard, alerted by the commotion in the hall, came limping out of his library to see his father pacing the floor.

'I am pleased to see you, Papa, but you have given me no notice of your arrival and Amy will not be ready to receive any visitors for an hour or so. She takes a nap after feeding time.'

'It's not your wife I came to see, Charlie.'

Charlie was not a man nowadays who took any rudeness or uncouth behaviour from anyone. He saw the opportunity to stand up to his father's blustering. He reckoned he had been a dutiful son, but now he had a son of his own, and had to reset his relationship with his father.

He was blessed with a wife he was most pleased with, and an heir — which still seemed like a miracle to him after thinking his chances of having a son and heir had vanished when on the battlefield of Waterloo. He had been pursuing orders from his father for all his life, but now he felt his duty should be to his wife. And waking her after a strenuous morning of childcare was not the best time to let his father see her — or his heir, her babe, sleeping in his cradle under the watchful eye of the nurse.

Charlie shook his father's hand, saying, 'I see you have already organised my maids to make you a fire up in the drawing room. So let us wait in there.'

Charlie spoke with such authority that the earl blinked and opened his mouth say something he then decided not to say. Evidently his son was not going to allow him to rule in his home.

The earl allowed Charlie to escort him into the drawing room and seat him near the fire, which was banked high with kindling, and throwing out sparks as well as warmth.

'How is Mama?' Charlie said, taking a chair opposite his father and stretching out his long legs in a relaxed manner, taking care to place his injured leg in a comfortable position.

'Humph! She ain't any better.' The earl's signet ring sparkled on his finger as he stretched out his hands to warm them near the blazing fire.

'I don't suppose she is.' Charlie smiled.

'But she wishes to see her grandson. You are to come and bring him soon, she said.'

Charlie chuckled. 'Of course, and so we shall, in a few weeks' time when Amy is ready to travel.'

'She'll not like having to wait a few weeks.'

'I dare say she will not, Papa, but remind her how she felt after giving birth to me — I doubt she would have wanted to jaunt about in a coach.'

The earl looked up at his son's stern eyes, and rubbed his chin.

The butler came in and served refreshments in exemplary fashion, which gave the travel-worn Earl the opportunity to enjoy his food and drink, after which the old man lay back and began snoozing.

Charlie chuckled and, leaving his father, galloped upstairs to see his wife.

★   ★   ★

Amy looked tired but blissfully happy, seated in bed with an infant in each arm.

'I expect you have heard my papa arrived a few hours ago, wanting to see his son's heir?'

'And Matilda, too?'

'He does not know about her. He is only interested in our boy, William.'

Amy sighed with a smile on her lips. 'I see I need not have bothered to have two babes . . . '

Charles sat on her bed close to her and taking her hand kissed it tenderly.

'The twins are for us, Amy. A girl for

you and a boy for me. Both are precious, like valuable finds we brought back from our honeymoon.'

Amy laughed, thinking of the day they were conceived in the hay barn when they were being chased by Lenoir's men. A frightening time. But it was worth it, as they had got to know each other during that dreadful time.

A life of luxury would suit her perfectly well from now on, and seeing her children grow and learn skills would be a delight for her.

'Charlie,' she said shyly. 'Do you love me?'

He caught her face in his hands and gazed into her deep blue eyes.

'Why Amy, of course I do!'

She sighed happily. All the moments of tenderness they had shared together were not, as she had supposed, from him obeying his powerful father, but because they genuinely cared for each other.

Looking at her babes she hoped that when they grew to adulthood, they too would be able to marry people they loved.

* * *

Meantime, the earl awoke downstairs.

'Where the devil has my son gone?' he shouted. He was tired of waiting downstairs after he had awoken from his map. Still trying to rule the roost, he saw nothing wrong with doing exactly as he liked in his son's house.

He was about to learn otherwise.

The butler came in immediately to remove the refreshment tray, and told his lordship that the viscount had gone upstairs to the nursery.

'Then take me up there!' the Earl of Collingwood ordered the butler.

'You may like to use the water closet first, sir,' the butler suggested.

'The what?'

The butler explained another new invention that Lord and Lady Chard had installed in their home.

'Whatever next? Show me this damn

confounded thing, then!'

The earl had to admit it was ingenious.

'My lord and lady have the latest of things,' the butler said, rather proudly. 'The cooks have the newest ovens and the kitchen is full of marvellous gadgets.'

'Well, I suppose it is Charlie's house, and he can do as he likes.'

'Just so,' the butler agreed, offering his arm to assist the earl up the grand staircase.

The Earl of Collingwood seemed to feel his age as he puffed and slowly climbed the stairs to see his daughter-in-law and her child.

His puzzled expression on seeing two babies, instead of the one boy he was expecting to see, amused both Amy and Charlie. But his delight was also obvious.

'Your house is full of surprises!' he declared.

Then he produced a silver rattle for William, and said Mathilda would have to make do with a kiss until he could buy her a gift.

'I have presents for you, too,' the earl said, turning to the proud parents. He rummaged around in his coat pocket and brought out a small box for each of them.

Amy opened hers to find a beautiful pearl necklace.

'Oh!' she cried in delight.

'Let Charlie put it around your neck, my dear. My old hands are cold and will make you shiver!'

Charlie brushed aside her long, neatly combed hair and carefully clasped the necklace around his lady's neck.

Amy felt the softness of the gleaming pearls.

'Thank you, sir,' she said sincerely.

Then her husband opened his small leather covered box, which he noted had the badge of the same jeweller on it. Inside was a gold ring with his initials on it.

'There you are, Charlie. Your own signet ring. I thought you would never want to wear mine again after all the trouble it caused you.'

Charlie slipped his beautiful new signet ring on his finger and looked at it with pride.

'You are right, Papa. You always are.'

'No — not always,' his father corrected him with a sudden rush of humility. 'But we are the commanders of our houses and estates, Charlie — which includes training the young.'

'I hope I will not be as demanding over my children as you have been with me!'

The earl's eyes twinkled as his eyes set on the infants slumbering in their mother's arms.

'You wait until your two babes grow old enough to get into mischief — you will set them straight.'

They all laughed, recalling their youthful follies.

The joyous occasion was interrupted by the butler tapping on the nursery door.

'Luncheon is served,' he announced.

Two aproned child nurses came in behind the butler and took the babies away from their mother. Amy rose and went to her room, where her maid prepared her for her lunch, while Charlie helped his father downstairs into the dining room and the seat nearest the fire, which almost suffocated Charlie with its heat.

When she appeared Amy was in her afternoon dress, now able to wear the clothes she had had made in Tunbridge Wells, although with her corset not laced too tightly. She had selected a stunning rose-coloured silk gown.

Goodness me — me, dressed in silk! she thought as she remembered the patched-up muslin dress she had been obliged to wear when her sister was being prepared for marriage. She wondered whether Harriet possessed such a luxurious garment as she now did.

After luncheon, Amy persuaded her father-in-law to stay the night. She had rooms always prepared for visitors, so deciding on the best one for him was not difficult.

★ ★ ★

That night, after a late dinner, the sleepy Earl Collingwood was happy to retire upstairs with the help of the servants. He found the guest room bed more comfortable even than his own, as he was put to bed in one of the guest bedrooms with a huge fire in the fireplace, the décor chosen by his daughter-in-law, pleasantly stylish. He fell asleep on the best bed and mattress money could buy.

Charlie, glad to get to bed himself, told Amy how genuinely pleased his father had been to see his grandchildren, and how he had received a shock to realise and accept that his authority over Charles had now altered.

His position in the family had altered by being a grandfather and he realised he would have to leave his son and wife to get on with their own lives. Although the old earl's wife, like Amy's mama, would expect them to bring the children to visit often, so that she could enjoy seeing her grandchildren.

Charlie also told her his father had said he was a lucky chap to have such a beautiful wife and children, and Charlie had told his father that he had earned his good fortune and position.

The words Amy cherished most of all, though, were those that Charlie uttered next . . .

'I am so happy that we married, my Amy — not because it suited me at the time I asked you to become my wife, but because now I know for certain that I love you — love you dearly and truly.'

Amy declared that she never felt happier, and they sealed their whirlwind love with a lingering kiss.

We do hope that you have enjoyed reading this large print book.

Did you know that all of our titles are available for purchase?

We publish a wide range of high quality large print books including:
Romances, Mysteries, Classics
General Fiction
Non Fiction and Westerns

Special interest titles available in large print are:
The Little Oxford Dictionary
Music Book, Song Book
Hymn Book, Service Book

Also available from us courtesy of Oxford University Press:
Young Readers' Dictionary
(large print edition)
Young Readers' Thesaurus
(large print edition)

For further information or a free brochure, please contact us at:
Ulverscroft Large Print Books Ltd.,
The Green, Bradgate Road, Anstey,
Leicester, LE7 7FU, England.
Tel: (00 44) **0116 236 4325**
Fax: (00 44) **0116 234 0205**

Other titles in the
Linford Romance Library:

WINTER GOLD

Sheila Spencer-Smith

Recovering from a bereavement, Katie Robertson finds an advertisement for a temporary job on the Isles of Scilly that involves looking after a housebound elderly lady for a few weeks. Hoping to investigate a possible family connection, she eagerly applies. But the woman's grandson, Rory, objects to her presence and believes she's involved with sabotaging the family flower farm. With an unlikely attraction growing between them, can Katie's suspicion of the real culprit be proved correct, and lead to happiness?